The Red Ribbon of Time

A Novel

The Red Ribbon of Time

A Novel *by*

Maria Menico Sifniades

BELLAPAIS PRESS
New Jersey

First US Edition

Photos of Bellapais Abbey – Maria Menico Sifniades

Author Photo by Maria Menico Sifniades

Cover and Book Design by Alexis Siroc Design

ISBN 978-0-9915796-3-1

www.writercooksgreek.blogspot.com

By the Same Author

Archangel

Acknowledgments

My debts to people who have helped me on this journey are many. Here, I single out a few, but my thanks go to all who lent their assistance to this writer.

I'm grateful to Jim Ryan, Maria Serghiou, Nelly Tsonopoulos, Louisa Mavrommatis Tzionis, for their helpful feedback on the early drafts of this story.

Thank you to Kathy Klauser, Karen Marcus and Joanne Atlas for their thoughtful reading of my manuscript. Thank you to my loving Godmother, Thea Geotas, for reading my manuscript and giving me her feedback and support. Stamatis Kampanis, I am grateful for your input.

To my friend Heather Caldwell, thank you for proofreading my manuscript with so much care.

I would be remiss not to express my gratitude to my wonderful cousins Efrosini Fraggou and Kaety Fraggou, who have accompanied me on my bittersweet pilgrimages to Bellapais Abbey, revisiting our ancestral lands while I researched this book.

Milda M. Devoe was of great help in editing the manuscript and I thank her for that.

And finally, I want to thank my wonderful husband, Stelios Sifniades, whose insights and support have been invaluable, as always.

AUTHOR'S NOTE

This is a work of fiction, and all the characters are imagined. Some historical events, however, are real:

Venetian-ruled Cyprus fell to the Ottomans in 1571.

Turkey invaded Cyprus in 1974 and is still in control of over 30% of Cyprus territory.

Bellapais Abbey and its history, dating from the time of the Lusignan kings, are real. The Abbey is in the area of the Republic of Cyprus that is currently under Turkish occupation.

This story was inspired by the author's ancestors, who descend from the last Frankish owners of Bellapais Abbey in the village of Bellapais in Cyprus.

In this novel, history is not fixed, but transformed into a living space that is fluid and open to negotiation; a place where relationships can cross the boundaries of time, across the centuries and transform into spirals and mandalas that are erased and reborn.

The story is inspired by the Frankish, Venetian, Ottoman, and contemporary history of Cyprus. Timelines and events may have been changed to enhance the storyline at the discretion of the author. This is a work of fiction.

Contents

	Prologue: Netta, Present Time	1
1	Annie, Bellapais 1571	6
2	Netta, Present Time	11
3	Annie, Bellapais, June 28, 1571	15
4	Netta, Present Time	23
5	Netta, Present Time	28
6	Athanasios, 1550	34
7	Thanos, Present Time	45
8	Annie, Bellapais, June 1571	49
9	Cyprus, Present Time	55
10	Annie and Athanasios, June 1571	60
11	Netta, Present Time	70
12	Annie, July 1571	74
13	Annie, July 1571	77
14	Netta, Present Time	82
15	Annie, July 1571	90
16	Netta, Present Time	93
17	Athanasios, August 1571	99

18 Netta, Present Time 102
19 Annie, July 1571 108
20 Athanasios, August 1571 112
21 Athanasios, September 1571 118
22 Annie, July 1571 121
23 Athanasios/Ioannis, 1571 127
24 Annie, July 1571 132
25 Athanasios/Ioannis, 1572 140
26 Netta and Thanos, Present Time 148
27 Annie, 1571 154
28 Athanasios/Ioannis, 1572 162
29 Annie, 1571 171
30 Netta and Thanos, Present Time 179
31 Annie, 1571 185
32 Athanasios/Ioannis, 1574 191
33 Netta and Thanos, Present Time 195
34 Annie, 1571 197
35 Athanasios/Ioannis, 1591 203
36 Annie, 1571 209
37 Annie, 1571 216
38 Athanasios/Ioannis, 1614 230
39 Annie, 1571 233
40 Annie, 1571 237
41 Annie, 1571 to 1623 242
42 Netta and Thanos, Present Time 246
43 Netta and Thanos, Present Time 258
Bellapais Abbey Photos 261

Dedicated to the memory of my mother, Eftyhia

Prologue : Netta

PRESENT TIME

Netta's sandal caught on the uneven ground of the courtyard. Finding her footing, Netta looked up at the towering Gothic arches that framed the gold-hued, limestone Abbey that had been part of her visions since childhood. Visions that haunted her sleep ever since she could remember. Visions that were hard to explain where they came from or why they visited her in the night.

She glanced at the church entrance under the arcade to the right. As she walked towards it, a large-scale fresco set in the recess above the transom of the massive wood doors came into view. An enthroned Virgin Mary with the Christ child in her arm was set in an azure background that evoked the magnificent color of the sea in the distance below. Only fragments remained of the painting. The Christ-child's face, still intact, a halo framed his head. Over the Virgin's right shoulder peeked the white wing of an archangel, and the mostly untouched by time archangel to the left, his sword drawn, appeared ready to protect his important charges.

Netta's mom, Eleni, had spoken of this fresco with longing in the rare times she spoke to her daughter about the place of her birth. Netta felt the importance of this woman in the fresco, evidenced by the scale of the painting and its placement at the entrance outside of the church. She now saw why her mom had such a vivid recollection of it.

She crossed the threshold into the stone church. Her eyes took a moment to adjust to the darker interior as cool air enveloped her body. She inhaled the sweet perfume of centuries of honey wax candle-burning, mixed with incense.

As she stepped down to the center aisle, a peculiar emotion welled up inside her and she felt the hair on her neck rise. A gauzy image flashed in front of her eyes: a bride, a handsome groom, a priest placing crowns over their heads in front of the altar. Chants of Byzantine psalms whispered in her ears and the scent of lemon blossoms mixed with fresh incense hit her nostrils. An overwhelming sense of joy formed a faint smile on her lips. Instinctively her hand flew to her bag, feeling through the fabric with her fingertips for the object that had kept her company since her mom gave it to her as a child.

A visitor bumped into her. The vision vanished.

"Wow, that was so weird," she mumbled to herself walking further into the church, her footsteps echoing on the time-worn marble. *There must've been so many beautiful weddings here in the past*, she thought.

The tall templon ahead held framed icons. In its middle stood the ornate Beautiful Gate with its fiery griffins guarding the Holy of Holies. Her feet seemed to know the way as they led her to stop in front of the icon of the Holy Mother. In this depiction, the Virgin wore carmine red robes and a gold crown sat on her head. The baby Jesus snug in her arms. Netta had the sensation that Mary's eyes were following her. Her sacred lips wanted to part to share a secret.

The eeriness of the moment did not scare her, but instead intrigued her and made her want to explore further. An icon of Jesus stood to the right of the Beautiful Gate and next to that was an icon of the Creator. In the furthest icon, which also served as a side door to the altar, a life-size Archangel Michael was depicted, with body armor on his strong torso, an enormous sword in his raised hand, and massive white wings on his shoulders.

Netta studied the crimson reds of his cape, the golds of his armor and the sapphire blues of the sky. She marveled at the long-ago artist who had created the masterpiece that was so evocative it made her heart ache.

The faint light from the hanging votive played against the angel's blue eyes. As with the Virgin, she had a feeling he was watching her.

Tearing herself away from the gaze of the Archangel, she walked to the other icons on the templon.

Slivers of sunshine stole through the narrow windows and danced off the crystals of the enormous chandeliers aloft. They chased each other on the stone apses of the cavernous church, this enchanted church of her ancestors she knew so little about.

It had been a lifelong dream of Netta's to travel to faraway Cyprus. Her mother, Eleni, grew up in Cyprus, in this very village of Bellapais that Netta was in now. Eleni had been twelve when the Turks invaded Cyprus. She and her family had fled to escape through the mountains to safety. Alas, the family had been ambushed along with other civilians by Turkish soldiers and Eleni had been the lone survivor. Rescued by the Red Cross, she was soon adopted by Grammy and Papa Johnson and brought to America. Her mom was reluctant to talk about what had happened. Netta first heard her mother's story when she was in high school.

I wonder if mom's feet ever stood where I'm standing right now, Netta thought, closely examining the splendor of the wood-carved throne to the right of the altar. The sculpted birds looked like they were about to take flight, and vines intertwined into the rest of the piece. The dark burnished wood showed centuries of wear and the domed throne was crowned by a cross. Eagles perched on each corner. Her hand reached up to stroke the marvelous object. She wanted to feel the feathers on the wings of the birds, the thorns of the vines, but the stern look of the guard dissuaded her.

She walked back towards the templon and turned left. There, she discovered a small chapel with a giant stone urn in the center. Netta recalled photos of Orthodox baptisms where similar urns were used to baptize babies. She circled the urn, appreciating the generous size and the graceful curves. She noticed the duller spots on the handles decorated with eagle heads betraying centuries of baptisms.

"Probably mom's baptismal urn," she thought and inched closer to the ancient relic. A strong need to reach for the urn rose inside of her. If she could only touch it, connect with an important relic from her mom's life, for even a second, she might unlock Eleni's hidden past, the childhood she never talked about.

While the guard was preoccupied in another part of the church, Netta reached for the urn.

As her fingertips contacted the cool stone, she let her palm caress the surface, as if caressing a beloved. A feeling of closeness with the child her mother once was, that child whose life Netta felt was kept hidden in the shadows, swept over her. And something surprising, a sense of belonging here, of being here before, rose and merged with the lifelong visions she'd had of this place.

"No touch!" the stern voice of the Turkish guard startled her. She grudgingly withdrew her hand and stomped away, stopping for a glance back at the urn that tugged at her heart.

1: Annie

BELLAPAIS, 1571

Annie's blond tresses lay loose across her pale white shoulders. Marina, her lady's maid, was carefully passing an ivory comb through her hair. The warm breeze gently blew the scent of lemon blossoms through the arched window. Annie inhaled the aroma deeply and gazed at the valley below and the sea beyond. Evening was falling and the sun played off the azure Mediterranean waters. The sparkles glistened like diamonds, and she felt as if she could reach out and gather them in her small hand.

Her mind wandered to Athanasios, her betrothed. He, the son of a Premonstratensian, the white robed monks of Bellapais, and a Greek Cypriot noblewoman; she, the great granddaughter of a Lusignan, a clan of Kings. They'd known each other for as long as they could remember, playing together as children in the Cloister.

"Run, I'll catch you!" he'd said, like he'd said many times before, since they were children.

"Aren't we a little old for that?" she'd retorted with a coy smile.

"No, we're just old enough," the young man whispered, and Annie started to run in the Cloister, giggling. Athanasios followed, giving her a wide lead. He didn't want to catch her in the Cloister where everyone could see them. He was already seventeen and she was turning into a young woman, her body filling out.

He chased her past the refectory and then down towards the kitchen and the Abbey's subterranean cellars. He loved to go down there and walk through the underground vaulted rooms filled with stores of wheat, olive oil, wine, nuts and whatever freshly slaughtered meats were slated for the meals. Annie led, her giggles echoing in the cavernous chambers, Athanasios chased her amid the slanted looks of the kitchen staff.

The two of them had free range of the Abbey as children, but now that they were growing older, it seemed as if people might not be as amused as they once were to see them frolicking. Annie was beloved by the Bellapais Abbey inhabitants and Athanasios was her constant companion. No one ever dared reproach them. They darted through the ceramic urns filled with food and finally emerged at the other end of the cellar at the back door that led out to the path leading to the orchards and the Vasiliki fields.

As soon as they found themselves alone on the deserted path, Athanasios sprung and grabbed his prey, making her laugh even harder. He pushed her gently against the limestone wall, encircling her in his arms. Annie's giggles stopped. She wrapped her arms around his head and stared into his eyes. Athanasios dipped his head and sought her lips, which she willingly gave.

Henri, Annie's father, had strongly discouraged the feelings they had grown to have for each other. They had to sneak to dark corners of the Abbey to see each other. Athanasios wouldn't dare ask for her hand.

But times were changing. The clouds of war were in the air and uncertainty had softened the strict societal rules governing whom one was allowed to wed. Henri had realized that Bellapais would need strong, young blood to defend it from the Ottomans if they laid siege upon it. In any case, the Abbey had fallen on hard times, and Athanasios' family money could go a long way in maintaining some semblance of propriety with maintenance of the buildings and payments to servants.

When the Venetians recruited volunteers to fight off the Ottoman raiders in Famagusta, Athanasios joined. His valor and fearlessness distinguished him so much, that he was awarded a knighthood by the Venetian Order of Chevaliers.

Upon his return to Bellapais, he had immediately sent his mother to bring his wedding proposal to Monsieur Henri, Annie's father.

Henri was no longer a young man. Against all conventions, though society rules discouraged a Frankish noblewoman's marriage to a Greek commoner, even one knighted for valor, he gave his consent.

The weight that had plagued her ever since she had realized that her love for Athanasios might never be fulfilled, lifted off her shoulders. What she had wanted for most of her life, to spend forever with Athanasios, was no longer a dream. She and he would be wed. Just when she had despaired that her dream would never be realized, her father had inexplicably relented and gave his blessing. Annie and Athanasios were to be married on June 30th, 1571, in the Church of Bellapais. That was where both her parents and grandparents were wed. It was March thirty- first and the preparations for their wedding were underway.

Yards of silk were ordered; the seamstresses were charged with sewing her wedding dress. Animals for the meal had to be fattened. Musicians had to be secured. Plenty of wine had to be stored. It all had to be ready for the wedding.

Amid all the preparations, Athanasios was called back to Famagusta to help fend off a new Ottoman raid. Annie anxiously awaited his return. Distinguished as a strong fighter, Athanasios had been instrumental in winning many battles. Annie was aware that her betrothed would throw himself wholeheartedly into battle, pursuing glory and ignoring mortal danger. News was hard to come by; men would seldomly be spared from the battlefield to bring news home.

"Look, milady!" Marina, her servant, pointed towards the sea.

"What do you see, Marina?" Annie snapped out of her reverie and focused on a dark spot in the horizon, the horizon she woke to every day and went to bed with every night. Whatever the dark spot was, it had never been there before.

"A dark cloud."

Annie peered ahead.

"You have a sharp eye, Marina."

"Thank you, milady."

"What do you think it is?"

"An armada, milady," the young woman replied.

"An armada?" Annie's heart sank. Her gut told her this dark mass did not portend well for Cyprus, for Venice, or for her.

She rose from her dressing table and hurried through the corridors, down the stone stairs, through the Cloister, towards her father's quarters.

Advisors spilled out from her father's rooms, and she spied him standing at the grand arched window facing the sea. His first lieutenant held a glass to his eye and gestured steadily ahead. The worried looks of her father and the hushed tones of his conversations with his advisors left her with the feeling that things were not going well. His pale face stopped her. She wrapped her arms around her shoulders, suddenly cold.

A little voice inside screamed silently.

"No, not my man. Not my love!"

In her heart she knew that something had dangerously, irrevocably shifted in their world. Her happiness was in grave danger.

"How selfish of me," she whispered. "So many people are in danger and all I can think about is myself."

Still, it seemed to her that the ominous cloud heading their way was an arrow aimed straight at her heart.

2: Netta

PRESENT TIME

Netta vividly remembered the only photo of her mother as a young girl. Mom was sitting in the grass smiling. Her small body was framed by intricately carved Gothic arches in the background. Her dark brown eyes shone with the lightheartedness of childhood and her brunette mane cascaded over her small brown shoulders. A white summer dress set off her tan and she looked so comfortable that Netta could tell that this was a place where her mom had belonged. The photo sat in a frame on the sideboard in the dining room, and Netta loved to study it.

"Mom, was it like Snow White's castle at Disney?" she would ask when she was little. "Did you live in a castle, mom?"

"It was an Abbey, Netta, something like a castle, but no, it wasn't a castle. I didn't live there but I sure spent a lot of time playing there."

"It must've been so much fun." Netta would say dreamily, running her finger tracing the squiggles of the arches.

"It was, that it was." Eleni's voice responded. "Don't ever forget, my darling," she would always add. "That Abbey is part of your heritage; it belongs to your ancestors. When you grow up, you'll understand better."

"I won't forget, mommy," the little girl would say.

What she didn't tell her mother was that the Abbey in the photo had invaded her dreams and transported her there at night. She ran through the magical ruins, the arches always present, towering over her. In the dreams she was carefree and happy. Oftentimes there was a little boy chasing her. They would laugh and giggle, and just as he was about to catch her the dream would end, and she never got to see his face.

As she grew, she asked her mother where the Abbey was.

"In Bellapais," she said," where I was born."

"Where is that? Florida?"

Mom laughed, that sweet almost sad laughter that Netta found so endearing.

"No, not in Florida. In Cyprus, an island far away."

"Take me there!" Netta demanded, hands on little hips.

"Oh, darling," Mom caressed her cheek, "it's so hard to explain. We can't go there, not now." she would say.

"Are you crying mommy?" the little girl asked.

"I'm fine. Come, let's put the photo away and play a game," Mom would say and wipe the little fingerprints off the glass, before placing the photo carefully back on the sideboard. She'd then start chasing her around the room making monster noises.

By high school, Netta knew very well where her mom's island was situated and talked about it to anyone who would listen.

"When I have enough money, I'm going to visit Cyprus," she would say to her friends.

The kids in school had never heard of it. She pinned a map she'd gotten by mail from the Consulate of Cyprus in New York City, on her wall. The booklets that were mailed with the map gave her a good overview of the history of the island and she knew that one day she would somehow get herself there.

When, at sixteen, she'd got her working papers, she got a job at the local pizzeria, saving half her earnings in a bank account her mom helped her open. "My Abbey money" she called it. It wasn't much, ten or twenty dollars each paycheck. No matter what she lusted after, whether it was the latest jeans, phone, shoes, or apps, she never touched her "Abbey money."

At seventeen, she really wanted an iPad, and her mom wouldn't get it for her. She'd said money didn't grow on trees and Netta's dad, who now lived in another house with his new wife and new child, was not inclined to buy it for her either. Everyone in school had one, except her.

Netta went as far as taking the money out of the account, but at the last minute, the dream of Bellapais was stronger than her desire for the iPad. Back into the account went the "Abbey money" and she started saving separately for the iPad.

It was during her sophomore year in college that she solidified her plan. The coming summer would probably be her last opportunity to be away for a long period of time before graduation and a full-time job. With three thousand dollars in the bank, she could finally travel. Plane tickets were bought, accommodations were arranged, luggage was borrowed, and all that remained was for her flight date to arrive.

Netta took her finals and immediately went shopping for summer clothes for her trip. Cyprus had a hot and arid climate, so she bought light tank tops and pants, a few pairs of shorts and a summer dress. Two bikinis and a straw hat completed her list.

She was to fly to Larnaca airport and be met by her mom's cousin who lived in Limassol, a shore town about a half hour drive away. Netta would stay with her for most of her four weeks on the island. Mom was driving her to JFK and her dad had even sprung for a new backpack.

"I want you to be careful while you're there," Eleni kept cautioning Netta. "At the first sign of trouble get on a plane home."

"Oh mom!" Netta would reply with an eyeroll. "Don't be so weird about it."

"Just remember what I said." Eleni would reply.

As much as Netta felt Eleni's anxiety, she also sensed her mother's excitement. It was clear in the way she talked about the food, the beaches, and the Abbey, as Eleni helped prepare for her daughter's first visit to the island that had borne her.

"Mom, come with me!" Netta had urged.

"I can't my sweet," her mother said. "You know I can't leave work. But you'll tell me all about it when you get back."

3 : Annie

BELLAPAIS, JUNE 1571

The fires in the mountains had been burning for days. Ashes sometimes reached Bellapais and painted the tips of the tree branches and edges of its rooftops in white like a faint sprinkling of snow.

There had been no news from Athanasios and the other chevaliers, and the Cloister was in deep turmoil. The fires that lit the night skies kept advancing towards the village and the Abbey. The armada, now clearly seen from the Abbey, flying the red flag with the three encircled yellow crescents of the Ottoman Empire, sailed just outside the Port of Kyrenia.

Annie's father and his men had not slept in days. The situation was the worst it had been since the beginning of the Ottoman raids.

Annie had been advised by her father to sequester herself in the Abbey and not venture outside the walls. That was hard for the young woman who had grown up wandering daily down to the orchards and fields of the Vasiliki below the Abbey, gathering wild herbs for her salves and ointments. Her mother had died during childbirth and her grandmother had taken her with her on her treks harvesting the medicinal herbs, as soon as she could walk. It was their little secret, she had told her at the time. The Church frowned upon such endeavors. It had to be a secret, lest they be accused of witchcraft.

How she wished her grandmother was still alive. She missed her a lot since she'd been gone, but now even more. She longed for her soothing touch and her sage advice. And she could really use some advice right now.

What was happening with Athanasios? On the eve that would have been her last night going to bed as a maiden, instead of trying on her wedding dress and reveling with her friends, she had been cowering in her chamber, choking from the smoke and fear.

A knock came on the door.

"Come in," she said.

Marina, her maid, appeared at the threshold.

"I brought some warm mint tea and rusks, milady." Marina set down a tray.

Annie stared at her and sighed.

"Thank you, Marina. Any news?" she simply asked.

Marina shook her head.

"Your father and his men are huddled in his chamber."

She walked over to Annie.

"Don't worry, milady. He'll come for you. I know he will."

Annie couldn't hold her emotions in check anymore and threw herself in her maid's arms.

Marina, a young woman not much older than Annie's sixteen years, brushed her lady's hair away from her face and gently caressed her cheek.

"He'll come." She soothed her. "I know he will."

After she calmed her lady down, Marina helped her to bed.

"Will there be anything else?"

"Thank you, Marina. I've been going out of my mind. Nothing else."

Marina gently closed the door behind her as she left.

Sleep finally came as a dark angel that took her hand and led her deep under his spell. Charging hordes of Ottomans, faces contorted into snarled mouths, eyes fired with rage, and arms raising their *yatagan* swords high to hack off the heads of the infidel Cypriots, crowded her dreams. She frantically searched for Athanasios in the mayhem, anxiously crouching in the shadows of a castle she did not recognize, amongst throngs of fleeing people. Smoke from fires burning everywhere burned her eyes and screams from mothers clutching babies and bloodied men dealt blows from the Ottomans, deafened her ears. Athanasios! Her mouth moved but no sound came forth. Athanasios! She couldn't hear herself calling out his name.

Just before sunrise, Annie gave up on her troubled sleep. She looked out of her window and glimpsed the rose dawn, a sliver in the horizon at the edge of the dark velvet sea. Grandmother always rose at this time, grabbing little Annie from the throes of slumber, dressing her quickly and stealthily walking her out of the Abbey to catch the first rays of the rising sun.

It had become a ritual that bound the two, even after Grandmother's death, one that Annie still observed.

The stillness of the hour imbued a calming peace inside her, and without it, Annie didn't know how to begin her day.

She and her grandmother would wrap their dark cloaks tightly around themselves and together they walked quietly across the courtyard and to the North side of the Abbey. They would bypass the outdoor kitchens that would soon begin to smoke with the fires of breakfast. They would sneak through the cellars stocked with massive clay *pithari* jars that held the Abbey's stores of olive oil, olives, salted meats, wheat, and dried fruits. The vaulted ceilings were hung with drying oregano and mint. They took the narrow path downhill towards the orchards and the fields of the Abbey. The morning dew on the weeds would dampen her cloak and shoes, the smell of the moist earth would hit her nostrils and the silence of the hour just before dawn would make her spirit soar.

Grandmother led her by the hand when she was very small, but soon she could tumble down the path behind Grandmother on her own.

They would follow the path as it ducked beneath the cliff where the stone walls of the Abbey, with their powerful buttresses, loomed above. Grandma held aside draping vines to reveal the low entrance to a stone cave. The air immediately got cooler, the smell of moss and wet stone hit her nose, and a gurgling foretold the spring that flowed constantly from the rock into a cistern. Three moss-covered stone arches framed the cistern in the musty cave. Grandmother rolled back her sleeves and dipped her hands in the cool water to wash their faces.

"This is like rosewater, so pure, filtered through the rock and flowing here for us to enjoy. Never forget that this is part of your legacy. I used to bring your mother here, when she was a child," she would say wistfully, anointing the girl's soft skin with the spring water. She was pensive, but just for a moment.

A wicker basket hung in the crook of her arm, filled with squares of cloth and a hunting knife in its sheath. She'd dampen the squares of cloth with running water and return them to her basket.

"Come child, let's continue, we have work to do before the Abbey awakens." And she'd lead Annie out of the cave and further down the path to the fields. Annie couldn't wait until they got down to the thick orchards where orange trees stood shoulder to shoulder with lemon trees, where gnarled trunks of olive trees grew to the size of dark giants, where plum trees and myrtle bushes lined the terraces. This was the place of wonder, where Grandmother began her work and Annie watched very carefully.

Depending on what grew during the season, they used the knife to pick oregano, sage, bay leaves, thyme, chamomile, basil, and mint, as well as aloe and anise. Careful to rouse any snakes that might have lurked in the brush before reaching in to begin her cuttings, Grandmother waved a long stick back and forth in the weeds.

Annie delighted in the svelte geckos scurrying away from Grandma's reach and, occasionally, the lone chameleon, a magnificent beast with a crest of horns and darting eyes, disturbed from his hunt by the thrashing about of the stick.

In the summer they collected yellow or deep orange calendula flowers to be dried and made into infusions to treat sores or rashes. They also used them to cleanse small cuts, burns and scratches. It was especially sought after for babies because it was delicate and soothing for their sensitive skin. Louiza, the floral lemony scented plant, was also taken for infusions to treat problems of the stomach.

Nettle, abundant in the Bellapais fields, was also harvested for teas to relieve bone pain and to promote a release of fluids. Grandmother used it to strengthen the child in pregnant women and to relieve female symptoms. She'd say that nettle tea was a woman's best friend. Annie learned early to keep her little body away from the plant, as its leaves and stems had little hairs bearing a sting that lasted days.

In the spring, they would pluck the magnificent white flowers of the *Zampoukos*, the wild elderberry plant. Annie loved the delicate scent of the flowers. Grandmother said that the flowers made a wonderful poultice for the skin, and many ladies sought this remedy so their skin would be free of blemishes. In the late summer, the dark berries of the plant were harvested for medicine and for food.

In the height of summer, they would harvest Herb of Saint John, the delicate yet powerful golden-yellow flower that held the spirit of summer within its fire. Not only was it beautiful but also magical with an abundance of healing powers. In an infusion, it was a powerful healing medicine that turned women's menstruum to a brighter red color. As an oil infusion it would specifically be useful as a rub for pain and as a healing of the skin from cuts, wounds, and grazes. The tincture would be used as a warming remedy, to calm nerves and to relieve the person of a melancholy state.

Of course, the plant that held the biggest mystique and was the most powerful and magical of all, was the Belladonna, the toxic nightshade. The beauty of its flowers belied the deadliness of its sap. Handled properly, it could be used to relax the muscles and relieve pain. Grandmother was very careful in the way she handled the Belladonna cuttings, and she taught Annie how to use the same care when it was time to let her begin the cutting and processing of the herbs. A miniscule amount, slipped into a drink, could send a person into paralysis, convulsions and worse. The reputation of the Belladonna as the poison of Kings made it especially important that Annie kept grandmother's secret about their activities with the herbs.

They would wrap the cuttings in the wet cloth so they wouldn't dry out and place them in the basket.

In the early spring, the scent from the orange and lemon blossoms was intoxicating. Annie could feel it invading her nostrils and traveling to her brain where it performed some alchemy, producing a euphoria that she relished but couldn't explain.

The women of the Abbey would set up a glass and copper still over an olive-wood fire in the kitchen yard. They brought baskets brimming with blossoms and took turns dumping them into the still. A glass bottle placed under the cannula was draped with a fine clean cloth. Once the vapors of the blossom water began to condense, they would drip through into the bottles.

Annie couldn't wait to get her own fresh bottle for the season. Her maid would pour a few drops in her silver wash basin in the morning wash-water and clean Annie's face from the night's sleep. But Annie also loved the blossom water in the Easter cookies it perfumed, and the rice flour puddings that transferred the fragrance of the orchards to the dinner table.

The properties of blossom water were well known, it was widely used in cooking and baking, as well as in washing the delicate skin of babies and young girls' faces. There was no need for her grandmother to produce any of her own.

Once Grandmother harvested enough cuttings and before the sun rose into the sky, she gathered her things and led the way back up the path. Back at the Abbey, Grandmother bypassed anyone up at that hour and carefully brought her cloth-covered basket to her personal rooms for further processing.

"Annie," Grandmother would always say. "What we do with the herbs and plants stays between us."

What Annie realized as she was growing up was that there were those in the Church who didn't look kindly on women interfering with God's ways. Grandmother's salves and poultices, teas and extracts, were widely sought after by those who needed treatment for an infected limb or a fever that wouldn't go away. Many women with swollen bellies secretly came to seek help from grandmother. But it all had to be done in secrecy, lest the Church men found out and accuse her of heresy. Not even her powerful son-in-law would be able to save her then.

People would often send a maid to beg for a potion or a tea or whatever treatment Grandmother decided, to bring back to an ailing Master or Mistress.

Annie had learned her grandmother's secrets by the time she was a teen. Now, in the privacy of her rooms and under the cloak of dawn Annie continued the family tradition of healing. Father knew, he had to have known all these years, but he turned a blind eye, satisfied that his people could find remedies when all else failed them.

The memories of her grandmother's morning ritual kept Annie company as she prepared her basket and quietly crept outside the Abby walls, against her father's admonitions. It was the only thing she knew that could calm her jarring nerves.

4: Netta

PRESENT TIME

Delta flight DA124 taxied along the tarmac at JFK before accelerating for takeoff and just like that, Netta felt the massive jet lift off into the air. She had flown once before but on a smaller plane and a shorter flight. This enormous airplane was new to her, setting her on a course filled with mystery and excitement.

The stale cabin air mixed with the smells of jet fuel unsettled her stomach, but only for a short while. From her window seat she could peer out at the New York cityscape below. As the plane circled above the city and headed east over the Atlantic Ocean, the massive skyscrapers looked as if they were made of Legos.

Once aloft, the captain came on the loudspeaker and talked about their flight time of seven hours to London, the fair weather, and that dinner would be shortly served. Smells of microwaved food hit her nostrils and she was surprised to find that she was hungry.

As she unfolded her tray table in front of her, she thought about her connecting flight from Heathrow to Larnaca. Yes, she had studied the online map of the airport, but it still was an unknown place. She was nervous about finding the right terminal to catch her flight. Three hours between flights seemed like plenty of time, but her nerves were, nevertheless, on alert.

As the flight attendant reached across the passenger next to her and handed her a food tray, her mind wandered to Larnaca, her destination. By the time she'd arrive at two in the afternoon local time, it would be six o'clock in the morning in the U.S. Jet lag, she thought, would be a new experience. She'd read about it, this effect on the body when you fly from one time zone to another.

Earlier in the week, Mom had contacted her favorite cousin, Sophia, about hosting Netta. It was arranged that Sophia and her daughter, Toula, would be meeting her at the airport. Netta was to stay with Sophia and her family and use their place as her base to travel around the island. Netta had spoken with Sophia and Toula over Skype, and she had been taken with how familiar both women felt to her, with their dark brown hair and dark eyes, evoking mom's complexion. There was joy in her mom's eyes as she spoke in fluent Greek with her cousin, something Netta seldom saw her do. They'd said goodbye, with Sophia assuring Eleni she'd look after her daughter. Netta had especially liked Toula, who'd promised they'd have a lot of fun together.

A sudden drop of the plane startled her, and she found herself gripping the armrest and looking around at the other passengers in the cabin. The movie was suspended, and the pilot's voice came on the loudspeaker asking everyone to return to their seats and make sure they fastened their seat belts. "Oh great," she thought. "Any more bumps like this and they'll have to pry my stiff fingers off the armrest to get me off this plane." Most people around her were asleep, which was oddly reassuring.

The plane steadied itself and Netta resumed watching her movie. The next thing she knew she woke up to the flight attendants serving coffee and croissants and the pilot talking about landing within an hour.

She drank the dark coffee, made bearable by the creamer and three sugars. She wolfed down the limp, soggy croissant, her thoughts to her carry-on, stowed above her head, worrying about how she'd get it down in time to leave the plane.

From her window she was excited to watch the plane descend flying low over London. The Thames River and what she thought was Big Ben were like a toy city below her.

"Awesome," she smiled.

The plane hovered over the runway and the wheels touched down jerking a bit and shifting the plane from side to side. When it came to a stop, the passengers immediately unclipped their seat belts and bolted, retrieving their carry-ons and other belongings. Netta did the same and was lucky a young man reached up and lowered her carry-on to the aisle.

Following the herd, she rushed off the plane, searching for info about her connecting flight. She spotted a screen and located the gate for her British Airways flight. Once on board waiting for takeoff, Netta's anticipation mounted. Cyprus was now within her reach.

Four hours later, the plane descended over a brown landscape before landing on the tarmac. The dry heat hit her in the face immediately as she exited the plane to board the bus to the terminal. It was a strange welcome to Cyprus.

Netta walked out of customs dragging her suitcase and carry-on, her eyes scanning the barricades for her relatives.

"Welcome Netta!" She heard her mom's cousin Sophia and her daughter Toula call out as they ran towards her. They ignored her outstretched hand and folded her into their embrace. Sophia's soft body smelled like warm bread and comfort and Toula's had a sweetness and freshness.

Nothing had prepared her for the heat once they stepped outside the air-conditioned terminal. The two women grabbed her bags and whisked her to the waiting car, where a man sat at the wheel.

"Uncle Harry," they introduced him, and he gave a broad smile and enveloped her hand in his large one.

Once inside the car they drove to Limassol, the shore town where many of her mother's relatives had found refuge after the invasion. Sophia kept stealing smiling glances at Netta and Toula reached out to hold her hand.

These are my people, Netta felt strongly, there was no doubt about it.

At the house, dark-haired, twenty-four-year-old Fivos emerged smiling from his room, the fourth member of the family.

A feast awaited at her aunt's house, set with *pastitsio*, the traditional pasta dish like lasagna she loved so much, *kleftiko*, the oven roasted lamb dish, salads, cheeses and lots of beer laid out on the back patio overlooking the small yard.

Even though Netta was just shy of twenty, no one asked whether she was of legal age to drink, and her uncle poured her a frothy glass of the local KEO beer that she enjoyed with everyone else.

"Eviva!" The toasts kept going all afternoon, until even her hosts could see that Netta's eyes were half closed, and she desperately needed to go to bed.

Her aunt led her to the room she would share with Toula, with two neatly made twin beds and a dresser in between them.

She fell asleep fast in the crisp sheets that smelled of lavender and roses. Her sleep was filled with strange scents and odd noises, mixed with dreams of dark-haired, brown-eyed people engulfing her in warm, sweet-smelling embraces, welcoming her home.

5 : Netta

PRESENT TIME

It was already 10 o'clock in the morning when Netta looked at her watch on the dresser. She'd slept almost twelve hours! She glanced over at Toula's empty bed.

"Good morning," Sophia chimed when Netta walked into the kitchen.

"I overslept," she blurted.

"Coffee?" Sophia smiled.

"Yes, please," Netta said, taking a chair at the table.

"You look so much like her," Sophia said with her back turned, stirring the Greek coffee in the small copper pot on the stove.

"You're her spitting image when she was young."

Netta surmised Sophia was talking about her mom.

"We grew up together, our houses so close to each other, we played all day." She placed the demitasse cup in front of her and poured the fragrant, frothy coffee in.

"Was she a happy child?"

"Oh, yes, your mom was always singing, always laughing. Her parents had no other children, so they doted on her. Eleni had all the good toys, but she always shared with me."

Sophia sat down, clasped her hands on top of the table and let out a deep sigh.

"That is until the war."

Netta's heart leapt. Mom never talked about those times. She longed to know the details that had transformed the sunny girl under the Gothic arches to the somber woman she knew as her mother. One look at her aunt's faraway gaze and tight lips dissuaded her from pursuing that conversation.

There'd be time later, she thought.

"Well," Aunt Sophia rose from the table. "Breakfast?"

Toula and Fivos walked into the kitchen, and soon Netta was bombarded with questions.

"What kind of music do you listen to in America?"

"What's school like in America?"

"What kind of phone do you have?"

"What apps are you using for travel?"

The chatter took her mind away from Gothic Abbeys and war.

As far as she could tell, Toula and Fivos had no summer jobs, they were college students on break. They talked about camping trips on the beaches of Cyprus, music clubs and hanging out with friends at local cafes sipping frappes.

"You have a job?" They both exclaimed when she talked about working at the pizzeria and then getting a job at the information center at school.

"Yeah, almost every student has to have some kind of job. I paid for this whole trip myself," she said. "You don't work?"

"We're studying so hard during the year that our parents want us to rest in the summer and recharge our batteries."

"Nice gig if you can get one," she said, and they looked at her with puzzled faces.

"Gig?" they said.

She laughed and went on to explain.

After Sophia's big lunch, the heat of August rose and Netta didn't protest when Sophia said it was time for a siesta. Was it normal here to nap in the middle of the day? She plopped on the bed next to Toula's, her eyes mid mast and took out her phone. She had a travel plan, but she was saving that for the road. Wherever possible she was going to use Wi-Fi.

Oh, mom! She remembered that she hadn't called her mother and immediately pressed the Facetime app.

Mom's morning face came on the small screen.

"Hi mom," she waved. "I'm in Cyprus, I still can't believe it!"

"Hi Netta," she waved back. "I thought you'd forgotten me now that you're on your adventure," she half joked.

"Yeah, right, like I can forget about you with all your relatives around me," she returned the tease.

"How is it so far? I mean, I know you just got there and everything…"

"Hot, it's really hot and, can you believe it, everyone is taking a siesta in the middle of the day!"

"I forgot to tell you about that, I almost forgot all about taking siestas."

"Me, Toula and Fivos are just hanging out in our room, but I can sure see why you could use a siesta, especially after those huge lunches."

Eleni started laughing and Netta gave her a squinty look.

"I'm not laughing at you sweetie. It's just funny to see my Cypriot culture through your American eyes. Cypriots eat their main meal at lunch. Dinner is just something light."

"Oh, yeah? You should have seen the dinner that Aunt Sophia had ready when I arrived. Wait, I took pictures. I'll text you some."

"That's 'cause you were an arriving guest, silly, and they wanted to do something special. They don't usually eat like that."

"Life is so different here. You know Toula and Fivos have never had a job?"

Eleni laughed again and then sighed.

"I gotta get some sleep before I go to work sweet pea."

"You should have come with me," Netta said.

"Maybe. But now I have to catch a train to work. Mwah," she sent air kisses.

"Bye mom, talk soon."

Netta leaned back on the bed and went through her Instagram feed for a while until she couldn't keep her eyes open anymore and surrendered to her nap.

Toula's voice shook her from the deep slumber she'd fallen into.

"Hey sleepy, you ended up liking our napping custom, he, he!"

"Oh my god! I really did sleep, didn't I?"

"Get up, we're going to meet some friends at a café."

"Do they speak English? How am I going to talk to everyone? Or know what they're saying?"

"Everyone speaks English,"Toula laughed. "Most of us have studied in England, so English is spoken here."

"Good," Netta said and turned to her side, eyes still closed.

"We'll take our showers, get dressed and go out. By the way, tonight we're invited to a beach party."

"Really," Netta sat up.

"Yes, really. Should be fun."

Netta got up and started rooting through her suitcase. She picked out a top and pants and fresh undies and headed for the shower. Inside the bath she noticed there was no place to set the showerhead on the wall so she could let the water rain over her. How was she going to wash her hair holding on to the showerhead with one hand and washing with the other? So different from home.

It took a long time for the water to heat up and when it did, it was way too hot. Netta couldn't hold the showerhead over her head while shampooing, and she couldn't lather and rinse. Frustrated, she found a way to perch the showerhead under her arm and washed herself the best she could.

"How on earth do they do it?" She wondered.

She got out and dressed, dried her hair and put on some light makeup.

Toula fussed a bit with what to wear, "does this make me look fat," "what brand are those pants you're wearing?"

The girls were ready to go and Fivos picked them up in his mom's car and they drove to the Limassol shoreline. In recent years it had undergone a major transformation. Netta's cousins explained that a pedestrian corridor had been created so people could walk for miles by the shore.

They could pick any café to spend the late afternoon sipping coffees and chatting.

The Café at the Amathous Hotel was something out of a magazine photo shoot. Long flowing drapes framed the outdoor sitting areas. Comfortable couches and armchairs made nice niches for groups of people who were sipping coffees from demitasse cups or frappes and frappuccinos from tall, frosted glasses. Colorful cocktails filled martini glasses and, from what Netta saw in the small plates, little nips of food and desserts she'd never seen, that looked like pieces of art, graced the tables. This was no Starbucks.

Her cousins started waving at a group nestled under one of the pergolas. Three young women with long dark hair and large almond shaped eyes and two tall, lean, young men waved back and beckoned.

Introductions were made but it was hard for Netta to keep all the names straight. Daphne, Aphrodite and Avgi, as far as she could remember, but who was who would take a while.

6 : Athanasios

1550

The Premonstratensian monks that inhabited the Bellapais Abbey had long abandoned the celibacy oath of their order and had taken wives from the local women of the village that had been growing around the Abbey.

George, who'd lived in the Abbey since early youth, had noticed a Greek Cypriot girl during vespers one evening. Her dark, almond-shaped eyes drew him in.

George spied her black curls peeking from the scarf that framed her soft white face. A Venetian fan held in her hands cooled her flushed cheeks. In all his life, he thought he'd never witnessed anything lovelier.

"Pay attention, my son," the priest admonished him.

The night seemed endless, perhaps it was the heat; possibly it was the girl. He saw her again the following night, and then the next.

George tried to avoid looking for her, but he found himself seeking her out. As he held the incense sensor for the Abbot at the altar, he found his eyes meeting hers. She held his gaze for a moment and then modestly lowered her lids. He continued to stare, admiring her arched eyebrows, her long dark lashes, her ruby lips. At her side stood an older woman, clad in rich silks and adorned with rows of Byzantine gold coins. Another young woman was in their party, dressed plainly in modest, aubergine-colored clothing: her maid, he presumed.

The next morning, he began to make discreet inquiries about the girl and her family. Her name was Margarita and Hadjisavvas, a wealthy Greek, was her father. He had but one daughter and two small sons. Young, suitable, Greek Cypriot bachelors were hard to find. With the plague, the Ottoman raids, the Venetian levies, not many young men were left. Would Hadjisavvas deign to consider a monk as a worthy suitor for his daughter?

His order was sworn to service and to poverty. Some of his brother monks had taken wives and had their own family quarters in the monastery. Their offspring could be seen playing on the grounds and roaming the Vasiliki orchards, often mixing with the village children in their daily games.

The Vasiliki orchards produced large quantities of fruit, olives, carobs and grapes. Large fields produced wheat and feed for the animals. The Premonstratensians were not poor. Maybe he had a chance.

As soon as the Dismissal Hymn's last words were chanted, George retreated to his cell to rest before heading to the refectory for supper. Before he had a chance to remove his white cape, Brother Nicholas showed up at the door.

"The Abbott requests your presence, Brother George."

"What's it about?" George was taken by surprise.

"I was not told of what he wishes from you. Just come with me."

George quickly followed the monk out of their quarters. It was highly unusual to be called to a meeting with the Abbott. George had only ever spoken to him twice before.

They hurried down the dark stone steps, following the flickering flame of the candle in Brother Nicholas' hand and sped through the long colonnade of the Cloister to the Eastern end of the Abbey.

George tentatively rapped his knuckles against the massive pine door left ajar, as the other monk slipped away.

"Enter," the Abbott's deep voice called from within.

"Frere George," the Abbott greeted him, sweeping his hand towards a chair across his desk.

"Your Holiness," George said, kissing the Abbott's hand in the customary fashion, before taking the seat.

The Abbott sat at his desk looking through a stack of papers in front of him. George searched his mind for whatever the reason might be that he'd been summoned. Could he have spoken too harshly to any of the other monks, did they discover that he'd eaten an extra biscuit last week when he was still hungry after supper, or did they think he had shirked his responsibilities when he only raked half the plot down by the vegetable garden? *I'll soon find out,* he thought.

"I'm going to get right to it," the older man finally spoke, looking up at George.

"Yes, Your Holiness," said George.

The Abbott sat behind an ornately carved wood desk with his head bare, his high hat with the peplum removed after vespers, a thinning braid trailing behind his back. The red velvet that covered the Abbott 's chair was of the richest fabrics George had seen, and the room the largest private room in the Abbey.

"Hm,hm. I heard you've been making inquiries about a certain local young woman."The older man looked him in the eyes. "Is that true?"

George had considered so many possibilities, but he hadn't expected his interest in Margarita to reach the Abbott's ears so quickly.

"Is this true?" the Abbott repeated.

George's ears were burning.

"Yes, your Holiness," he managed.

"What is your interest in this woman?"

George was completely embarrassed, yet he knew very clearly in his heart that his interest was noble and honest.

"I want to marry her, your Holiness."

The Abbott paused for a moment while his eyes searched George's face.

"I see," he finally said. "You are a Latin Novice and she, a wealthy Greek."

"I am aware, your Holiness." He lowered his eyes.

"Does the lady reciprocate?"The Abbott pressed on.

George hoped the dim light of the candle hid the crimson rising on his cheeks and traveling to color his ears beet red.

"Well, does she?"

"I don't know, your Holiness," George stammered.

"What do you mean you don't know? Have you spoken to her of your intentions?"

"No, sir!"

The Abbott tented his hands and leaned forward.

"Hm, hm," he uttered as he studied George. "The arrival of new novices from France has trickled to a stop. To keep this Abbey viable, we'll need to make compromises to continue the Glory of our Lord."

George held his breath. Could it be?

"If you plan to marry, we will provide you with quarters for you, your wife and your family to come. And an income from the fruits of our orchards. You will not be destitute. Bring your bride here."

George sat for a moment in silence, thanking God for looking out for him.

"I have never spoken to her," he finally said.

"Very well. We will help you, George. We will send word to the father then. Agreed?"

George shook his head in agreement.

He'd never expected this turn of events. In his heart, he knew that Margarita was interested in him the way he was interested in her. He knew by the way her eyes shone when she looked at him. But to marry? Would she agree to that? Most of all, would her father agree?

¤¤¤¤¤

Hadjisavvas had been following the Ottoman raids against the island very closely. He had sent his top consiglieri to town to bring back news. Cyprus had been under the Venetians since the demise of the Lusignan. They were no better than the Franks, as far as he was concerned, but at least they were also Christians. With the Ottomans, he just didn't know what would happen if they were to prevail.

As he was contemplating all of this, his servant came into the room and announced there was a visitor at the door.

"Who is it, child?" he asked the young girl.

"It's the Abbott, milord."

"What are you waiting for, then? Show him in!" He thundered.

Even though the Abbey was far from its old glory, the Abbott of Bellapais still enjoyed considerable respect among the locals.

The girl scurried away and returned to the living room accompanying the Abbott. Hadjisavvas rose from his seat and approached the holy man.

"Welcome to my home, Your Holiness," he said kissing the top of the Abbott's hand. Even though he was a Latin priest, he was still to be afforded the rituals of respect shown to Greek Orthodox clergy.

"Thank you, my son," said the old man.

The servant showed him to an armchair and Hadjisavvas waited for him to be seated before he took a seat across from him.

The two men looked at each other for a long moment.

"You must be wondering why I'm here," the Abbott finally said.

Hadjisavvas nodded.

The Abbott shifted in his seat and leaned slightly closer.

"It's a delicate matter."

Hadjisavvas dismissed the servant with a wave of his hand.

"Close the door behind you," he commanded.

"What is the reason for your visit?" Hadjisavvas asked as soon as the door clicked shut.

The Abbott took a deep breath and folded his hands carefully in his lap.

"It's about your daughter, Margarita,"

Hadjisavvas gripped the arms of his chair.

"What about my daughter?" he said.

"Please, don't be alarmed. I'm here for a good cause. You'll see, once we talk about it, I think you'll be glad."

Hadjisavvas relaxed his grip, but his face was still taut.

"What about my daughter, your Holiness?"

"I'm here with a proposal for your daughter," the Abbott finally said. "Margarita is a woman now, how old is she, seventeen?"

The other man watched him closely, his brow frowned.

"These are changing times, Hadjisavva,"

"Yes," he nodded. "Go on."

"I'm here on the behalf of one of my novices."

Hadjisavvas jumped from his chair.

"A novice for my Margarita?"

The Abbott regarded him calmly.

"Listen to me first, before you make any decisions."

"I am Hadjisavvas, well known to everyone in this town. Why should I even consider such a proposal? What can a novice offer her?"

"I understand your qualms, I didn't come here lightly."

"Well, then?"

"As I said, these are changing times. The Ottomans are circling the island. There is danger in the future. Margarita will be safer in the Abbey than in the village. She will never need for anything. The Abbey can provide for her, and we grow everything we need, and enough to sell. She will have her own quarters to live in with her family and any servants you give her."

Hadjisavvas' expression changed to one of interest.

"Go on…"

"You could always visit her at the Abbey and she you. If you marry her to someone from farther away, that will not be possible. Besides, if you ever need shelter behind the Abbey walls, you shall have it."

"And who is this man who dares ask for my Margarita?" Hadjisavvas asked in a softer tone.

"It's our novice George. I would never have come if I didn't know him to be hardworking, honest and brave. Your daughter could not fall into better hands, my son," the priest assured.

Hadjisavvas sat silent for a moment.

"Does he know my daughter?"

"He's seen her in Church from time to time. She's a beautiful girl and she shines among her peers."

Hadjisavvas leaned closer to the priest.

"Does she reciprocate?"

"That's for you to discover. If you decide that George is a good match for your Margarita, go ahead and ask her."

Hadjisavvas nodded.

"I'll think on that."

"That's all I ask. Think about it and give me your answer. Margarita's future will be safe and secure with George. I guarantee you that he will protect her with his own life."

The Abbott rose. The two men shook hands and Hadjisavvas escorted the honored guest to the door himself.

"What was the Abbott doing here, husband?" Hadjisavva's wife inquired later that morning.

Hadjisavvas took his wife by the elbow and led her to their bedroom, looking around for prying eyes and ears.

"What's so secret, Hadjisavva?" she asked as soon as the door shut.

He paused for a moment, as if he were trying to find the words.

"He was here for Margarita."

"Margarita? Our Margarita? What for?" she blurted.

"Ssh," he cautioned. "A proposal for marriage," he whispered.

"Oh, that's nice. She is young, but I suppose it's normal that she's attracting interest." She beamed. "From the Abbott?"

Hadjisavvas gave her a look.

"An Abbey novice," he said.

His wife's face fell, her eyes darkened.

"A novice for our Margarita! That's preposterous! Unbelievable. You did turn him down, didn't you?"

Hadjisavvas looked down at his hands.

"Hm, hm. Not exactly."

¤¤¤¤¤

George paced the Cloister at dawn, oblivious to the yolk colors of daybreak over the horizon. On his knees that morning, he weeded the vegetable patch, plucked the shoots from the tomato plants, and propped the cucumber vines in what felt like a trance.

Two torturous days passed in routine monastery life. Maybe he should have waited until he was certain of the feelings of his beloved. Waited until he could learn how friendly her father might be to the Latins. Waited until he was sure she would be his.

The Abbott, though, hadn't given him a chance. The issue of asking for her hand in marriage came up so quickly, George hadn't had time to strategize.

Yet, perhaps this had been the best way. Perhaps it was good to act swiftly while Margarita's interest was high and before her father could consider other suitors who would surely be coming her way.

Why was it all taking so long? Did the Abbott send his proposal right away? Was Margarita's father even considering him, or had he already been rejected?

George finished his morning chores in the field and sped up the path towards the Abbey. He couldn't stand not knowing anymore; he was going to ask the Abbott for news.

As he rounded the bend up from the Vasiliki, he spotted an entourage. Flanked by two young men, Hadjisavvas was advancing through the Great Door leading to the Cloister. Even from a distance, he saw how well-tailored their trousers were and the beautiful motifs of the embroidery on their tunics. Their dark capes flew behind them and their high boots shone of spit polish and expensive leather. On their heads sat flat hats, each adorned with a feather.

George couldn't help looking down at his muddy linens and moccasins.

"Oh, Dear Lord," he muttered, scurrying behind a wall. "Please don't let them see me like this!"

Peeking from the edge of the stone wall, George made sure the visitors were gone from his path before he emerged, running towards the monk's quarters.

And it came to pass that George did marry Margarita and they settled in the Abbey's quarters as had been promised by the Abbott. She came with her own maid, fine furniture and her father's blessing.

It wasn't long before their little boy was born.

They called him Athanasios; named after a Greek Orthodox saint, but also meaning immortal in Greek.

7: Thanos

PRESENT TIME

"Hi, my name is Taki," said one of the young men at the café where Netta and her cousins came to meet their friends.

"Netta," she replied, shaking his hand.

"Thanos," the young man next to him said, and she turned towards him.

"Netta," she replied and took his extended hand. A sense of calm and well-being immediately enveloped her, as if the hand holding hers was a wellspring of joy.

Taken by the sensation but somehow not surprised, she raised her eyes to his. *"How do I know this man?"* she puzzled. She was sure they'd never met before, yet he seemed familiar. How was that possible?

A vivid vision of a giggling little girl chased by a boy through an arch-framed garden flashed through her mind. The girl laughed and turned her head to see if the boy was close enough to catch her.

"Pleased to meet you," his voice brought her back. His grip tightened on her hand, and a cloud passed over his gaze.

Netta shook off the eerie feeling and gave Thanos an awkward smile. He let go of her hand and the group of young friends rearranged themselves around the low coffee table.

It was still hot in the late afternoon; Netta thought it was close to ninety degrees. Avgi, large brown eyes framed by thick eyelashes, shifted her seat to make room for Netta, and Taki brought her a chair. Soon a waiter showed up to take their order. The two girls ordered iced frappes, and Daphne, her long dark hair in a ponytail draped around her neck resting on her ample bosom, followed suit. Soon frappes were ordered by the rest in the group and Netta decided to try one. The tall glasses arrived with the dark coffee and foam on the top, a colorful straw set in each of them.

"As I'm in my last year at Edinburgh," said Avgi, "I'm looking for something in London. I'd love to work in the City, but I don't know. My grandparents have an apartment there, so it wouldn't be too bad, even if the salary is low."

"Yeah, me too," said Taki. "I'm looking for work in Germany. They need engineers there and a lot of my friends have already gotten offers from German firms."

"What about you, Netta?" Thanos addressed her.

Again, the familiarity of his voice confounded her. It was as if she'd known that voice from before. How could she know this man? It was surreal to have an ordinary conversation while feeling such a strong sense of déjà vu.

"I may want to go for a Master's," she replied carefully. "I'm studying history, so there's not a whole lot I can do, unless I just want to work as an assistant somewhere."

"What kind of job would you want to do as a historian?" Avgi interjected.

"My dream job would be working at the Met," she replied.

"The Met?" a couple of the friends asked almost in unison.

"The Metropolitan Museum of Art," she clarified.

"Ah, yes! I imagine that would be a great place to work. I've never been but I've heard of it."Thanos said.

"Are you interested in history?" she asked him.

"You can't be a Cypriot and not be interested in history."

"How's that?" she asked.

"Our island's history is so long and rich, we are always learning something new about it. Do you know that practically anywhere you dig on this island there's antiquities?"

"No," she said, embarrassed. "I never knew that."

"Oh, yes. Just the other day they dug the foundations for a building in the old Amathous area and discovered what they think are the remains of an ancient home. They've found an intact grave, complete, in addition to the skeleton, with all the votives that had been buried with the dead."

"Wow!" Netta exclaimed. "That's pretty cool."

"Most ancient graves have been looted. With this one, archaeologists might be able to study the ancient rites and forgotten customs."

"It sounds like you may be the historian in the group." Netta added with a laugh.

"He's also the smart one," Daphne said and patted Thanos' shoulder.

Netta thought Thanos may have flinched a little at that touch.

"Hey, are you coming to the beach party later?" Thanos asked.

Netta thought Daphne tightened her lips.

"Yes, my cousins mentioned it earlier."

"Great!" he said. Daphne turned her back and got involved in a conversation with Taki next to her.

Netta began to slowly unwind and got caught up in learning about the lives of young people in a country other than her own. She let go of thoughts about her job and school, about her mom and dad and let herself be carried away by the languor of the early island evening.

8 : Annie

JUNE 1571, BELLAPAIS

An intense feeling that someone was in her room woke Annie in her dark chamber. Sleep had been hard won that night, but this sense of strangers in her private quarters was not born of that.

Lying completely still, her eyes half-opened, she was waiting for the dark to turn to gray. Before her brain had a chance to fully register the figures by her bed, a hand had covered her mouth.

"Don't be afraid, milady," a man's voice said as Annie struggled, trying to scream, to summon help. Only muffled, failed sounds escaped her mouth.

Where was her maid, where were the Abbey guards?

"Mm, mm," she turned her head back and forth on her pillow trying to free herself from the intruder's hand.

"This is an emissary from Athanasios, milady," she heard her maid's voice.

"Don't scream, I'm going to take my hand away, but don't scream," the man's voice said.

Annie bolted upright in her bed as she was released.

"Marina, what is happening?"

"Milady, John has been sent by Master Athanasios to take you away from here."

Annie took a moment. Her pounding heart was reverberating in her ears.

"Why isn't he here himself?" she finally uttered.

"He's fighting the Ottomans in Famagusta, milady. There are so many more of them than there are of us and there are fears the city will fall," the man spoke.

"And what about you?"

Marina grabbed a large cloth and began to throw Annie's dresses, toiletries, and undergarments in it.

"What are you doing, Marina? How could you trust him, how do we know this is true?"

The man named John reached around his neck and removed a gold pendant. She grabbed it in her hand, still warm from John's body, and ran her finger over the contours of the piece in the semi darkness. It had been her gift to Athanasios for their betrothal: a medallion of his namesake, Saint Athanasios.

Pressing her lips together in silent acknowledgment, Annie put the pendant around her neck and allowed her maid to dress her for the journey.

"Milady," John said. "You should take your jewelry. Athanasios said bring anything of value. We'll try to get you to Venice."

John reached inside his shirt, drew out a folded piece of paper and handed it to her.

"What's this?" She looked down at the small parcel, sealed with a red wax stamp bearing the initial A. Her fingers traced the straight lines of the A, caressed the uneven contours of the wax seal, as if she were reaching over the mountains and the plains to the battlefield and stroking her beloved's rugged face.

She broke the seal open, unwrapped the letter, and tried to read in the gray darkness.

Marina rushed to light a candle from the torch outside the chamber.

My love, I write from the battlefield. The Ottomans have many more soldiers and ammunition than the Christians and we are fighting hard so they will not overcome our defenses. As of now, we are holding up, valiantly. I sent my friend John to take you away. I've secured passage for you to Venice. This is only to protect you in case the invaders overcome us and head for Bellapais. I cannot bear the thought of anyone harming your fair person. I swear to you on the Saint Athanasios medallion you gave me, that as soon as all this is over, and we throw the Ottomans into the sea, you and I will be united again, and our wedding will take place in the Abbey of Bellapais. I promise. I embrace you, Athanasios.

"It's true then..." she murmured, tears salting her cheeks.

Annie's strength abandoned her, and she dropped to the ground sobbing. Marina knelt beside her.

"Hush, milady, we must not be discovered. There's still a long road before we reach the sea where our boat is waiting. Be strong for your father and for Athanasios."

As if waking from a trance, Annie cried. "Father, what about Father?"

Marina's hand flew to her shoulder.

"We must leave now, before dawn reveals us to our enemies. Your father's place is here, with his people."

"Yes, milady. We left word for him with the night guard. We must rush. If Famagusta falls, it will be only a matter of time before they reach Bellapais. We must get you out of here before it's too late," John said.

Annie wiped her face and reluctantly rose to her feet.

"I must say goodbye! I can't leave like this without even kissing his hand and asking for his blessing."

"We can't risk anyone stopping us. We must leave before dawn. The old guard will tell him all he needs to know."

John stepped ahead and Marina tied the cloth into a bundle and hoisted it over her shoulder.

Reluctantly, Annie reached into the dresser drawer by her bed and removed a silver filigree box. She took the cloth bag that held her homemade remedies and herbs and draped its long handles across her body.

"Let's go." Marina said and took Annie's hand.

She pulled her mistress decisively out the chamber door and led her through the dark corridors, past sleeping guards and empty halls.

The three dark figures crept through the Abbey gate and walked towards the orange grove. A man with two saddled mules awaited.

He bowed his head slightly. When Annie reached him, he placed his hands around her small waist and lifted her onto one of the animals. Her maid hitched up her dresses and hoisted herself behind her.

John rode the lead mule. The guide followed on foot, leading the mule with the two women by its reins.

The trek down the mountain towards the sea was treacherous in daylight and perilous at night. The animals couldn't see where they were going and might easily be spooked by a night owl or startled by a darting rabbit.

Their guide kept a silent vigil and soon the only sound was that of crickets in the night and the clip clop of hooves on the rocky path.

Shifting in her saddle, Annie turned back towards the dark shadow of the Abbey. It loomed over the cliff, its enormous mass seeming solid and protective of all who resided within its walls. How could it be that she had to slip away in the middle of the night to save herself from the Ottomans? She glimpsed the life she was leaving behind, her father sleeping in his quarters.

Marina squeezed her arm, and the procession continued its somber journey. The mules clopped along overgrown paths of barbed bushes that snagged her dresses and feet, along olive grove orchards, whose limbs bore down to snatch her cloak. Annie had no time to feel afraid. The escape, Athanasios' pendant and letter, the dark Abbey, the journey down the mountain, were all too much to process, and her feelings were on high alert. She felt that if she just lifted her hands off the saddle, she might fly away into the dark and sinister night.

After about an hour, the group descended to the plain. Their guide expertly maneuvered the animals down a hill and along a creek full of tall reeds that ended at a small, pebbled beach. The pleasant June night and the calm sea belied the storm in her breast. Hushed conversation came from two men waiting behind the rocks. After a quick exchange of gestures with John and the guide, they wordlessly helped unload the women and their belongings.

A small rowboat hidden in the cove was dragged to shore and Annie, Marina and John boarded as quickly as possible.

"Go in the name of God," the guide said as he shoved them off and walked away to lead the mules back up the mountain.

Annie sat frozen in the wooden vessel amid her belongings. Marina and John said nothing. The waves slapped against the sides of the boat in a rhythmic foreboding dance. The salty air brought some clarity to her thoughts, and she touched the medallion at her bosom.

What if it was all a ploy by the Ottomans to get her away from the safety of the Abbey? They were known to kidnap girls and scurry them away to the Sultan's harems in the East. What if Athanasios had not sent word but had been killed and his pendant taken to be used to trick her? What if John wasn't who he said? What if Marina had been bribed to betray her?

What had she done?

9 : Cyprus

PRESENT TIME

The sand, still warm from the day, cradled her bare feet, radiating its heat from Netta's toes all the way up her body.

About thirty people milled around that stretch of beach, swigging sips from KEO beer cans, drinking brandy shots with Coca Cola and enjoying whiskey sours in plastic cups. A fire pit was set up in the middle of the strip and piles of wood had been brought down to the beach. The fire had been lit as soon as the big orange globe of the sun dipped into the sea, and it now blazed high into the ink night.

Netta was standing with a cold KEO in her hand talking with a young man who had been born in London.

"Oh, yes," he said. "The Cypriot community in London is enormous. There must be several hundred thousand Cypriots back home."

"What are you doing here then?" she laughed.

"The Cypriots are much less traditional here. It's like time stood still for my parents and their friends. They still hold tight to customs and values they brought with them when they left decades ago."

He kicked the sand.

"Here, the culture has evolved, embracing the modern world. I feel free. And there's the sun and the sea. You can't beat that," he laughed.

Netta laughed too.

"No, you can't. It's really beautiful. Everyone is so much more carefree than we are in the States. We're always working. Here, they're playing."

"You've got that right," he said and asked if she wanted another beer.

"No thanks," Netta said, and he walked towards the cooler.

"Hey there," someone tapped her shoulder.

She turned to find Thanos standing behind her.

"Oh, hi." She noticed how handsome his dark face was against his white shirt.

"Are you having a good time?"

"Yes!" she blurted. "This is the best vacation I can remember."

"Really? How so?"

"Well, I've been dreaming about Cyprus ever since I saw a photo of my mother when I was about four. It was in a garden with Gothic arches in Bellapais, her hometown," she said.

"Your mother is from Bellapais?"

Netta looked at him for a long moment. She followed the contours of his cheekbones to the wells of his brown eyes. The long eyelashes seemed to whisper a secret she couldn't quite decipher. His lips were well defined, full and determined, always ready to break into a smile.

"I hope we're not related. Everyone is somehow related on this island." He laughed but his eyes showed he was serious.

"I wouldn't know. My mom never talks about her childhood. It was a very traumatic time for her. The war."

"Yes, the war. That's all we grew up with here. We live our lives trying to forget that a third of this island is occupied by Turks who could expand South at any moment, and no one will stop them."

"That must be so hard," she said. His lean body seemed to tense up.

"Well," he looked away. "Let's talk about something more fun. You're here to have a good time, so let's get some more KEOs." He steered her towards the cooler.

Netta followed. Under the brightness of the Mediterranean sun lay a dark veil that she had never been able to lift. Not with her mother, nor her aunt. And now Thanos alluded to it, but when she came close to seeing beneath it, he pulled the curtain shut and closed her out yet again.

"Actually, I'm here to learn more about my mother and her past. I don't mind having fun and it's a great island to do that, but I've been planning this trip for years. I want to know."

He turned to her. "Do you really want to know?"

"Yes, I do."

"Tonight, we party. Before you leave, I'll take you to Bellapais." He handed her the beer, and they joined her cousins and their friends around the fire.

The sand between her toes was a sweet reminder when she woke up the next morning. She stretched her body long, feeling a sensuous languor. The party had been a magical experience. The dark sky, the calm sea, the people around her. And Thanos. She just wanted to lie still for a while and dream about Thanos with his brown eyes, his tanned arms and his handsome smile. The paradox was that when she was with him her joy was immeasurable, yet so was her sadness. It was hard to comprehend what was happening to her, even though she'd lived with strange feelings and sensations for a long time.

She turned to look at Toula, who slept deeply in the next bed. Netta closed her eyes and in her mind smelled the salty air of the night before. Reliving the experience of sitting next to the serious young man, she felt the tingling of their bare arms accidently brushing against each other. She smelled his musky aftershave and recalled his elegant hands wrapped around the KEO can. His presence had heightened every sensation in her body.

She sighed deeply and turned to her side. Toula stirred and opened her eyes to look at her cousin.

"Good morning," Netta said.

"Mmmm," Toula mumbled, from that place between wakefulness and sleep.

The two girls, still in bed, began to talk.

"So, where did you disappear to? I lost you for half the night." Netta said to her cousin.

Toula giggled and looked at her meaningfully.

"The one with the long hair?" Netta probed.

Toula nodded, still giggling.

"Oh, he's cute," Netta approved.

They took turns in the bathroom washing the sleep out of their eyes and the salt and sand from their bodies. They toasted some bread and sat down to cups of Greek coffee.

"So, what about you?" Toula gave Netta an eyebrow lift.

"What about me?"

"Thanos."

The girls laughed.

"What about Thanos?" Netta said, still giggling.

"He seems pretty interested in you."

"Really?"

"Don't tell me you haven't noticed. I saw how you spent most of the night sitting next to him."

"He's really nice. I like him. Sometimes I feel as if I've known him before. You know? Have you ever felt that way?"

Toula gave her a puzzled look.

"Where would you know him from? He's never been to America, as far as I know." Then she added, "Maybe from another life."

The two girls broke down laughing so hard they couldn't speak when Fivos walked into the kitchen.

"What are you two laughing about?" he asked, looking down at himself and running to check in the mirror.

10 : Annie, Athanasios

JUNE 1571

The boat bobbed in the dark sea, and the clouds overhead moved to obscure the stars. Annie laid her head on Marina's knees and tried to make sense of the events of the night.

Perhaps she had been too quick to believe John. She should have spoken to her father first, she could have been duped and abducted! She touched the corners of Athanasios' letter. There was no mistaking the seal. She silently wept in her maid's lap praying she was safe as John pulled the oars across the water.

Athanasios had left for battle over two weeks ago and no word had come from him during that time. This was the week of their planned wedding, a wedding she had longed for. Yet, her unlucky stars kept them not only apart at a time that should've been marked by great joy, but also put them both in situations of great peril.

Would she ever see him again? It was at least a two-day ride from Famagusta to Bellapais when John had seen him last. Was Athanasios still alive after two days of battle? If the Ottomans overpowered the Venetians, how would Athanasios even survive this battle? What about Father and the Abbey? Would they endure, and if not, would they have time to leave, would her father just stay behind and fall under an Ottoman sword?

These despair-filled thoughts swirled around her head with every stroke of the oar that brought her further from Bellapais. No one could predict what would happen, nor could she even know what her own fate would be going forward.

She had not been prepared for any of this. She had been raised in the bucolic lands of the Bellapais Abbey and, even though they were now under the Venetian rule, they still had more privileges than the Greek Cypriots living outside the perimeter of the Abbey. The fields belonging to the Abbey yielded enough crops to feed everyone within and to sell at the market for needed cash and taxes. Her father claimed that the old glory of the Abbey had faded, but she didn't see any of it. Life had been good to her; it had brought her her beloved, Athanasios.

Now, she was practically alone in a boat headed for God knows where, taken away from her familiar grounds and her loved ones. Had she been too rash?

Marina's hand softly stroked her cheek and wiped the tears as they ran down her face. Annie grabbed Marina's hand.

"Did we do the right thing, Marina?" she whispered in the salty breeze.

"I think we did, milady. John verified that he is your fiancé's emissary, didn't he?"

She continued stroking Annie's face.

"And the fires burning in the mountains are too much of a warning not to heed. It was the right thing."

Annie surrendered to the rhythm of the boat and Marina's caresses. Suddenly, she became terribly exhausted, and her eyes could no longer remain open. Soon, her breathing became shallow, and she dove deep into the murky waters of her subconscious.

The boat moved through the water under the cover of darkness, with John at the helm pulling the oars hard.

"Don't worry milady," he broke the silence speaking into the night. "I may be young, but I've already been tested in battle. I was the one he chose as his emissary because I'm his most trusted soldier." He looked at his charges in the boat.

"Don't worry, I won't let you down."

Several hours passed in silence, the two women having fallen asleep in a heap. John kept his vigil and, even though he had slept little in almost two days, he continued his route towards the cove. He had been rowing for most of the night. The only man on board, he knew the women were relying on him. The cove was a place that he had learned about as a child when he would spend the day fishing with other men. It had been a few years since he'd been there. With the cloak of night he had been unsure if he was on the right track, but he knew he had to keep rowing if he was to get there before the light broke in the sky. When the hills receded and the shore became almost even with the sea, John knew he was in the right place.

When he finally rounded the cove, his arms heavy from toil, he saw the women stir.

"Where are we, John?" Annie whispered.

"We are approaching land, milady," he replied.

"Are we in Venice?" she puzzled. "It seems impossible to have reached its shores in just a few short hours. Look, it's not even daybreak."

"No milady. We are still in Cyprus."

"What are we doing here, then?" her voice high-pitched with alarm.

"Calm, milady. I didn't tell you earlier because I wanted to be sure no one else knew of our plan. We are to meet Athanasios here."

He rowed the boat eastward towards the cape of Apostle Andreas in the Karpasia region, hoping Athanasios would be waiting to meet them there as planned.

Annie shifted her weight abruptly in the boat.

"Calm, milady, calm. We're almost there. See that fire on the shore? That should be your fiancé, waiting for us. We had made a secret pact to meet here. He will explain everything."

Annie searched the dark shoreline. As much as she wanted to believe John, she was still worried that she had been taken under false pretenses. Her heart beat hard in her breast. Suddenly, as the boat bobbed on the water, there was the light on the shore that John had promised. The light that lit her path towards her beloved.

The fire burned brighter on the land as the boat neared. Annie could make out two figures. Men. Was it her beloved or was it a villain who would be taking her and Marina to the slave bazaars of the Orient that women around the Abbey frequently talked about? Should that terrible fate fall upon her, would she have the strength to kill herself before any of it came to pass?

John was steady at the helm, steering them closer and closer to the shore and the men around the fire. Annie now could see a man that could be Athanasios, his body type almost identical to his, but this man had a full beard and wild hair running down his back. His clothes were worn and a sword draped across his waist. The other man looked like he wore a cassock, his hair in a bun at his nape and a black beard long over his chest.

She kept her eyes on the men as the boat travelled to shore. They ran towards the place where the boat was headed and Annie craned her neck to get a better view of the figures approaching. Her whole life depended on who they were.

Before she knew it, the boat had run ashore, and the men waded into the water and pulled it onto the pebble beach.

Two strong hands reached in and lifted her by her waist and carried her to the beach. She discerned the tired face of Athanasios behind the beard and the deep lines that now crossed it. His grip on her was so familiar that she let herself melt in his arms. When he set her down on the ground, the two of them faced each other silently for a moment. He kissed her face tenderly, wiping away the tears that streamed down her cheeks, and gripped her hands as if trying to make sure that she was there, on the beach with him.

"Athanasios! I was so worried for you," she cried out. "I missed you," she whispered.

"I missed you and worried for you too!" he echoed without taking his eyes off her.

The others stood discreetly by.

"I brought Father Vikentios," he finally said pointing to the man in the cassock. "Before you leave for Venice, I want us to get married. It's not the way we thought our wedding would be, but during these hard times we must do the best we can." He kissed her hand.

"Without Father? Without a wedding dress? It's not how I imagined it," Annie said softly.

Marina stepped up and stood next to her mistress.

"I will stand by you, milady."

John stood next to Athanasios. Father Vikentios donned his *epitrachelion* and produced a bible and a large gold cross.

"This will be a simple ceremony, but you, Athanasios and Annie, will be duly married in the eyes of God," the priest said, and Annie felt the truth of his words.

Athanasios took her hand and handed John two stone rings, tied together by a satin red ribbon. The priest told them that the red ribbon tying the wedding rings together symbolized the unbreakable bond between husband and wife. The connection could stretch or tangle but, regardless of place or time, the couple were forever destined to be together.

Annie and Athanasios stood side by side before the priest while he proceeded to perform the wedding ritual. The traditional wedding crowns, symbolizing the glory and honor bestowed on them by God, were fashioned from olive branches that were collected nearby. Father Vikentios placed them on the heads of the bride and groom, and John, as the best man, switched them back and forth between the two young people three times, invoking the Holy Trinity, as well as signifying that the couple's worth lies within each other. The priest chanting the incantations that would bind them in matrimony, placed the rings on the third finger of their right hand, and their bridesmaid and best man exchanged them between the couple three times, symbolizing the give and take of a happy marriage.

When the last prayers were said the priest pronounced them husband and wife. Annie and Athanasios held each other tight for a long time afterwards.

The yards of silk brought from Venice for her wedding gown, the bolts of lace for her veil, the barrels of wine and the fattened sheep for the bridal feast would remain behind at the Abbey. Annie was married.

"What do we do now?" Annie asked.

"We'll spend the rest of the night in a cave nearby where a friend has prepared bedding for us. In the morning, John will take you and Marina to meet the boat that will take you to Venice, where you will be safe. I will send for you as soon as the fight is over."

"No, I don't want to leave, I want to stay with you! We are married now. I go where you go."

"Shh," he soothed her. "We'll see in the morning."

"If we are to part again, I want you to have the pendant." She removed the necklace from around her neck and placed it over Athanasios' head, letting the pendant land on his broad chest.

"This will keep you safe."

"Hurry," the priest said. "It will be light soon."

Athanasios took his new bride's hand and led her along the coastline, keeping on an ancient path. Not far from where they were just wed, he dropped down a cliff-side and helped her scale the steep rocks.

"Where are you taking me?" she laughed. "I thought you said a cave, not a cliff!"

"Trust me," he said, and they continued down the cliff, her maid and John following at a discreet distance to keep guard over the newlyweds.

Athanasios now led her to a spot on the cliff, waters lapping underneath. He stopped.

A few yards down, he said: "Close your eyes!"

"Oh you!" she giggled. Even in the midst of war, her beloved had retained his playfulness. And she, still a girl, could forget for a moment the scene of her midnight exodus. She could put aside her thoughts of leaving behind her father and the only home she ever knew. She could be, if just for a few hours, a new bride.

He let go of her hand.

"Don't peek."

She stayed where she was, eyes closed, waiting.

She heard a sound like dried bramble been dragged, and then Athanasios pulled her by the hand.

"Open your eyes!"

Annie could now see that they were in a large cave, not far from the sea, but hidden enough by the side of the cliff to offer them sanctuary for their first night together. Marina and John had stopped several yards away, to give the newlyweds enough privacy, but close enough to guard the couple.

A fire was burning close to the entrance, and Annie could see that bedding had been laid on the floor of the cave. A flask of wine, a basket of fruit and a loaf of bread were also part of the Bridal Suite. A basin with fresh water was set beside the bedding.

Athanasios reached behind him and dragged the rudimentary bramble door to cover the cave entrance.

He then slowly approached his new wife. Annie stood still and waited for him to draw nearer.

He reached out his hand and stroked her cheek as she melted into it. He caressed her hair and gently pulled her to him. Annie's lips parted for Athanasios's deep kiss. He pulled her towards him and pressed his body on hers.

Annie let out a deep sigh.

"My darling!" he cried as he held her body and began to explore its curves.

He touched her the way she always dreamed he would. Athanasios had held back before they were married, telling her that he wanted to marry her first. Now, she was his.

He reached for the laces of her blouse. She trembled as he slowly untied and loosened them and pulled the fabric back to expose her young breasts. The look in his eyes when he beheld her naked body for the first time made Annie crazy with passion. She never imagined it could be like this.

She tore at his clothes, pulling every stitch off until they stood completely naked in front of each other. The flames of the fire gave their skin a warm glow. They tumbled onto the bedding set for their bridal night and nipped and tugged and grabbed at each other's flesh as if their hunger would only subside after they'd devoured each other.

When he entered her virginal body, she was ready to receive him, her whole being blossoming and rejoicing in their union.

"My love," she moaned. "My husband."

The hours passed too quickly, and spent, they fell asleep in each other's arms, relishing their love. Thoughts of their impending separation were temporarily pushed aside, making way for abandon and joy in being alive.

11: Netta

PRESENT TIME

Time in Cyprus passed so easily. Netta was surrounded by a welcoming family, and the languid warm days and the sultry nights were filled with outings with her cousin's friends. Thanos had become a regular companion. The feelings of déjà vu were often there, but she tried to shake them and go on with her present life. She'd thought about what her cousin Toula had said in jest. That maybe she'd known him in another life. Toula did not know of Netta's visions, she did not know of the world that had haunted Netta since she could remember.

Netta soon realized that it would be easy to fritter her summer away without focusing on the real reason that brought her to the island. The Abbey beckoned. On the nights that she lay on a warm beach somewhere on the coast looking up at the star-studded Mediterranean sky, or when she lounged at a café with her newfound friends, she longed to go there and experience its mystical aura. Yes, getting to know Thanos was a major draw of spending days following her cousins and their friends. Something about him pulled her into his orbit. He had offered, early on, to take her to Bellapais. The offer didn't come up again and Netta wasn't comfortable enough to bring it up.

And, yes, he was a puzzle to reckon with. But the pull of that ancient edifice, set in that photo of her mother on the sideboard at home, was inescapable.

"How do I get to Bellapais?" she asked her aunt at the morning table. Sophia's hands stopped chopping the onions for the midday meal. Her body stiffened just enough for Netta to notice that the question had unsettled her.

"Do I need to rent a car?" she persisted.

"Now dear, aren't you having a good time here with your cousins?" her aunt finally said.

"Well, yes, I am. A very good time."

"So why would you want to go there? It's on the other side of the Green Line where Cypriot soldiers are on one side, the UN in the Middle and the Turkish army on the other side. Maybe you should leave it to another time, on another trip when you're a bit older, maybe..." Sophia said not looking up.

Netta's chest tightened. Why was Sophia trying to discourage her? Sophia's tense body told her there was pain and anguish in that place. Yet, Netta knew that it was something she had to pursue. Somehow, the Abbey would unlock the mystery of her visions. She was sure the answer would be found at the Abbey.

"Aunt Sophia," she said gently. She understood how fragile the older woman was, "I need to go *now*."

Sophia sighed. She turned around, wiped her hands on her apron and sat down across the table from Netta.

"Okay then, child." She took Netta's hands into hers. "Okay then."

Sophia and her husband had agreed that they would drive Netta across the demarcation line, called the Green Line by the United Nations and the Cypriots, and into the Turkish occupied area of Cyprus, to their ancestral village.

Netta was standing in the driveway, watching her uncle checking the car oil the day before their trip.

"Toula will go with us tomorrow," he said as he looked up from under the hood. "Fivos will stay here, in case there's any trouble while we're behind Turkish lines. It's good to have someone in the Cyprus government-controlled area we could call to help us."

"I didn't realize it was going to be so complicated," she said.

Her uncle stopped what he was doing and wiped his hands on a rag.

"Netta, I don't come from Bellapais, but your aunt does. I didn't have to flee my village under Turkish occupation, like she and your mother did. But I did live through the Turkish invasion and, in the back of my mind, I can't trust that everything is going to be okay. What if something happens politically while we are there?"

"I guess you're right. I hadn't thought about that. But, so many people go."

He shut the hood.

"Yes, many people go and come back." He sighed. "Your aunt and I went once when the Turks first opened the barricades. She needed to go and see her childhood village," he said wistfully. "It was a bittersweet trip, with lots of good memories for her. She saw her house, her village, and her school. But it was bitter, because Turkish settlers lived in her house, Turkish settler children were in her school, and the orchards and ancient olive groves where the villagers grew their food, were replaced by villas with swimming pools for European buyers of their stolen properties. She cried all the way home until she couldn't see anymore."

"I'm so sorry. I had no idea."

"Didn't your mother tell you?"

"My mother never talks about it. There's only the photo of herself as a young girl among the Abbey arches that she keeps on the dresser. That's why I decided to come and see for myself."

The man shifted awkwardly from leg to leg. He wiped his hands again with a dirty cloth and looked at her somberly.

"You're not a child anymore, Netta. You should know that bad things happened during that war. Bad things happened to your mother."

Netta had long sensed that terrible things must have happened to her mother. But hearing the words out loud made it somehow real and utterly horrible.

"I thought something terrible might have happened to her there," she finally said. "I need to go there, I need to know about my family, my history, about my mother!"

The two paced around each other by the car, as if in a dance with slow, sad steps.

The man shook his head.

"Yes, you should know. Tomorrow, we'll take you there. You can walk the streets of your family's village, go to your mother's house and you and your aunt can talk about all the hard things that have not been spoken of all these years."

12 : Annie

JULY 1571

Annie stood at the stern of the Eleonora, leaning gently on the wooden gunwale as the land of Cyprus receded. The mountain peaks shrank away into the distance and each gust of wind that filled the sails served as another brushstroke to erase Athanasios, her father, and Bellapais from her life. As temporary as Athanasios may have made their separation seem, it was still a painful reality to her. As young as she was, she had enough sense to understand that she may never see any of them again.

Earlier that morning, their rowboat had stopped astern of the big galley waiting at sea. She and Marina had been helped up the rope ladder slung over the side of the ship by the sailors aboard. The captain came to greet her and ordered his second in command to escort her and her maid to their cabin. The galley was part of a group of ships that had delivered reinforcements and badly needed goods for the battle of Famagusta and was now returning to Venice. Athanasios had heard about the ships a month earlier and had developed the plan to whisk Annie to Venice for safety. Now, she was onboard, on a long voyage north through the Mediterranean towards the Adriatic Sea with Venice as the destination.

They said that it could take up to a month to reach the Serenissima, depending on the weather. Cyprus may have been called the Daughter of Venice, but the daughter was a long way from home. Having never made this voyage before, or any voyage at all, it all seemed extraordinary to Annie. If it weren't for her trusted John and her maid Marina, she didn't know how she would ever have had the courage to board that vessel.

Their quarters were a cabin with two bunks, away from where the men hung their hammocks to sleep the few hours that they were not on duty shifts. The groans of the boat's boards, lines and sails, straining against the winds' forward motion, unnerved her. It seemed that at each wave they scaled ahead, the ship was ready to break apart. The vessel climbed the wave and then dipped on the other side of it, giving it a rhythm that the first few days seemed so unnatural. Her body reacted violently, and she had to relieve her stomach's meager contents several times during the day and night in a bucket over the side of the bunk. Mercifully she had her trusted stash of herbs and made tea with calendula to soothe her body and mind.

There seemed to be no end to this torture. Once they were well underway, the winds picked up and the ship unfurled more of its sails and galloped forward towards its destination.

Venice was an unknown place, she worried that the arrangements made by her new husband might not materialize. The uncertainty and precariousness of her situation was beginning to hit her, and the more she thought about it all, the more desperate and frightening it all seemed. She had no one to consult besides her maid Marina who was a very loyal and good servant, but alas, she had no more experience of lands or circumstances outside their Abbey, than she. John, Athanasios' trusted friend, had proven to be also very loyal and protective of her. But she could tell that this was also his first voyage.

Marina and Annie spent their days sewing as much of her jewelry as possible into the clothes they were wearing, trying to hide and protect the only things of value they owned.

How she missed Father! So much had happened in such a short time, life-changing things that she would normally have shared with him. He would have rejoiced at her wedding, but not in the way it happened, furtively like outlaws in the wilderness in the middle of the night! She wished she'd had time to consult with him. Maybe she should've insisted that they stop by his chambers. Was he safe, she wondered? Had Bellapais been attacked by the Ottomans? Did they fight them off like in the past or did they succumb this time?

Every day at dawn, she came up to the ship's deck to stretch her limbs, inhale the salty air, and take stock of her surroundings. They were a week at sea and her body had gotten used to the motion. On the morning of the seventh day, she looked out from the deck to where the tip of Candia was receding from view as they left it behind to pivot north en route to their destination in the Adriatic Sea: the safety of Venice.

13 : Annie

JULY 1571

Shouting rang across the decks as the men scrambled to amass the limp sails that fluttered in the dull wind. Annie had felt the boat's speed slowing down when the ship changed course, headed North, en route to the Serenissima.

As she stood on deck the night before, prior to descending to the stuffy bowels of the ship where she slept, she had noticed the trembling of the sails and the lighter breeze that barely filled them. She had been on board a week and had gotten used to the ways of the winds that propelled that fantastical vessel forward. The shift was noticeable, even to a land person like her.

The oars on either side of the boat in the deck below her sleeping quarters, began to lift and fall, keeping the rhythm of a pounding drum that reverberated all over the galley. In that early morning twilight, she opened her eyes to noticeable activity aboard the ship. The oars still played their monotonous synchronized dance, but the crew seemed to be more alarmed.

She climbed out of her bunk and splashed some water from the bucket nearby on her face. After smoothing her unruly hair and running her hands over her wrinkled dress, she scaled the steps to the deck. No one noticed her. Everyone was busily walking around the deck, amassing heavy lines, checking the oars and looking out at sea.

Annie spied the captain, a tall, massive man with the long glass on his eye and his brow furrowed. The sailor beside him pointed aft at an object only they could see. Looking in the direction of his hand, she tried to discern what it might be, to no avail.

Soon, the speck on the horizon began to reveal to her the threat that it posed. It grew bigger and bigger and as fast as their ship tried to row ahead, away from this looming menace, she could see that they were losing space.

"What is she doing here? Get her below, at once!" The captain noticed Annie frozen in a corner of the deck, watching the frantic activity of the seamen, desperately trying to put more leagues of water between themselves and the ships that were on their tail.

Two rough hands grabbed her and ushered her below decks.

Annie practically stumbled down the hatch and ran to find her maid.

"Marina, Marina where are you?" she cried, struck by the realization that their situation, already precarious, was rapidly going to get worse.

"Milady," she replied running towards Annie. "What's happening on deck? We're going so fast, and I hear the crew yelling and scrambling."

Annie grabbed her hands and steadied herself before replying. Her thoughts were in shambles, and she needed a moment to formulate what was racing through her mind.

"Pirates!" she cried. "We are pursued by pirates!"

They looked at one another, both knowing very well, even though they had lived a sheltered life within the walls of the Abbey, what that could mean for them.

Marina's face crumbled. Fear burned in her eyes and her hands gripped Annie's tighter. Words could not describe what they felt, the terror that was upon them and the feelings of helplessness that crushed them. Would they outrun them? Would they be overtaken? Would the Captain manage to protect them from a terrible fate? She didn't know.

Marina and Annie crumbled to the floor and sat there in each other's arms; their ears focused on the sounds above.

They were the only women on board. John, their protector, had joined the crew aloft in trying to outrun the pirate ships. Annie's mind refused to contemplate who these pirates were and what would happen if they were to be captured.

"Marina," she shook the girl who whimpered in her arms. She held her close. "We're going to be alright."

As the boats in pursuit gained ground, the crew fought valiantly to outrun them.

The winds had shifted, and the galley was sailing against the wind. The oars rose and fell, yet the distance became increasingly smaller.

The pirate ships, smaller and more limber, loomed larger and larger until the moment when they reached the galley and shifted to go aside it and allow the pirates to board it.

Wild eyes shone in the light, betraying the crew's knowing that once those brigantines sided with their ship, their lives would not be the same.

The noise from the deck had gotten more frantic.

Annie let go of Marina and gathered her skirts to mount the hatch back to the deck.

"Where are you going, milady?" Marina whimpered.

"Get up, girl!" Annie commanded in a voice she hardly recognized as her own.

As much as she was raised a dutiful daughter, the sense that her life was in danger propelled her to defy the captain and act.

"We're going up on deck," she said. "From there we can see what's happening. Better to face the danger than to cower down here waiting for death to come to us like rats in a trap."

Marina's expression changed to one of puzzlement.

"Get up! If we're to die, we're going to do it standing."

Marina wiped her tears with the back of her sleeve and stopped crying.

Annie's tone shook her out of her helplessness.

She rose to her feet.

"You're right, milady,"

Annie strapped her medicine bag across her body and drew her cloak over her shoulders. Up the hatch they scurried, unnoticed by the frantic crewmembers who were fending off the pirates trying to board the vessel.

The two of them hid behind the main mast and a pile of ropes and watched.

A pirate leaped across the chasm of sea between the ships and landed on deck. Before he could get on his feet, a crewman of the Eleonora stomped a boot across his neck and struck him on the head with a club. The blood gushed from the fallen man's wound and both women flinched behind their hiding place. Next thing, another crewman ran his sword through a pirate swinging on a mast line. The screams were heart-wrenching, the blood was staining the decks, and the gun powder was exploding from the mouths of the muskets carried by the men on both sides.

Marina crossed herself and turned away to hide her face in her hands.

Knowing full well that their fate depended on the outcome, Annie could not avert her eyes from the scene.

Bodies flew in the air, men struggled body to body, large hands grabbed throats and threw punches. Swords pierced flesh and knives slit throats. In the chaos of the melee, she could not discern whether their side was winning or losing, as much as she tried to keep track of how many were overtaken and how many pirates had managed to board the Eleonora.

Through the haze of the battle, she saw the pirate ships completely sidle-up to their ship. Rough men, with black cloths wrapped around their heads wielding knives and pistols, boarded the Eleonora one after another as if they was an endless army. She let out her breath and tried to keep herself from panic and despair. It was well known, even to sheltered girls like her, what pirates did to women whom they captured.

One week earlier she had been in the bosom of her father, dreaming of the return of Athanasios and their wedding day. Things were bad and the Ottomans were at the gates of Famagusta, but she had such faith in the valor and strength of their men, like Athanasios, that she'd never dreamt that she would be whisked away in the darkness of night, marry her fiancé on a deserted beach at dusk, and board a ship for a perilous journey to Venice. None of those events were on her horizon. Yet, this surreal journey had gotten much worse. What was to become of them?

14 : Netta

PRESENT TIME

Netta's aunt came into her and Toula's room before dawn to rouse the girls.

"Mooom!" Toula protested and turned towards the wall pulling the covers over her head.

Netta flipped onto her back and stretched her body long. It had been a while since she had to wake up early in the morning to catch a train to work or classes, so she was kind of out of practice. Cyprus time was easy going and languorous. Easy to get used to.

"Girls, if you want to go to Bellapais, you must get up now. It'll take you forever to get ready, Toula. Come on, my sweet." She cajoled her girl, sitting at the edge of her bed and reaching out to gently pull the covers from her face.

"Oh, okay then! I'm getting up. What time is it, anyway?"

"Five."

"So early," Netta managed to say while trying to open her eyes.

"We have to be in the car by seven. This way we'll have all the time we want to spend walking around the village and visiting the Abbey before we head home before dark. I'm going to make some sandwiches and snacks for the road. I don't want to spend one cent more than I have to over there."

The girls finally got themselves out of bed and took turns showering and getting ready. It promised to be a hot day, so Netta wore a pair of white linen pants, a strappy top and her Tevas. She packed her favorite tote bag with some wet wipes, her little makeup bag, took her phone off the charger, packed her notebook and grabbed her red scarf from the chair where she'd tossed it the night before.

She checked her messages and saw Thanos's text asking to meet. She replied that she wouldn't be around because her family was taking her to Bellapais. "Another time?" she had texted. He gave her the thumbs up.

Toula emerged from the shower refreshed and wide awake. Fivos was left to sleep while the family prepared for their journey. Netta used the time the others were preparing to Google the distance between Limassol and Kerynia. She was surprised to read that it was almost seventy miles, from one coast of the island to the other. Bellapais was four miles further.

She had read that the island ran about 140 miles long at its longest point and 60 miles wide at its widest point. It covered a surface of 3,500 square miles with a coastline that was around 400 miles long. Compared to American distances, it was small.

By the time they were getting in the car, the sun had risen, and the day was already hot. The couple sat in front and the two girls settled in the back seat. The air conditioner in Uncle Harry's car wasn't working, so he'd turned it off and they rolled down the windows.

The warm breeze carried the smells of dried weeds and parched earth from the fields they passed along the road. Netta loved these new smells. They stirred in her some wayward memory, as if her brain was saying, I know this smell, I know this smell. How odd, she thought. Where could I possibly know this smell from?

It was kind of weird how they drove on the left side of the road, a relic from the British rule, but it all seemed to work just fine. The drive to Bellapais began on the highway that led back to Larnaca, towards the airport where she'd arrived only a week ago. Then, it veered north to Nicosia, the divided Capital of Cyprus. From there, they would drive to the checkpoint and cross into the Turkish occupied territory.

Netta had done her reading about Cyprus from the booklets, pamphlets and maps she'd received from the Cyprus consulate in New York. There was so much information, with the history of Franks, Venetians, Ottomans, British rule and Independence in the Twentieth Century, that she was sure she could not keep it all straight. And certainly, she was not alone in this, since the "Cyprus Problem" as it was internationally known, was one of the most intractable issues of the times.

By the time they got to the checkpoint, it was already nine o'clock and the heat was beginning to rise. Uncle Harry handed the approaching guard her passport and their Cyprus IDs, paid the car insurance fee to be covered on the other side, and continued on the road towards Bellapais.

The road was wide and new, with several buildings on either side. What was striking was that the Greek and English lettered signs were replaced by signs in what she presumed was Turkish. This made the transition immediate and real. A few miles in, Netta could see the mountain range towering in the distance that separated the Mesaoria plain from the province of Kyrenia, where Bellapais was located.

The drive was mesmerizing. The landscape was dusty and dry yet eerily intriguing. The tarmac shimmered from the heat as the car consumed the distance. The anxiety of what awaited them on the other side of the mountain was something Netta hadn't bargained for. She had been planning this trip for so long that her emotions were focused on getting there. Now that the trajectory was set, and she was hurtling forward, there was no turning back. Would Bellapais meet her expectations? What would she discover there? Would her mother's ancestral house still be standing? Would she find any clues about her grandparents, her family?

The four-lane highway wound around the mountains before it emerged on the other side. Netta thought she'd never seen a more perfect color blue than what appeared before her. A full view of the Mediterranean Sea lay ahead. The landscape changed from dusty to green, as if the climate on this side of the island, this side of the mountains were different. She watched as her uncle deftly navigated the road as they drove into the outskirts of the city of Kyrenia.

"Things have changed so much!" Sophia exclaimed wide-eyed. "I can't even recognize where we are!"

Newly built high risers flanked the highway, and buildings in the process of being built were interspersed amongst them, cement skeletons framed by wooden molding structures.

"Once we get to the center of town we'll know where to take our turn." Harry said.

The girls in back were quietly taking in the sites. Netta looked over at Toula and the girl reached out and took her hand in hers. She held on tight, and the drive continued.

They finally reached a more densely populated area, which seemed to be the center of Kyrenia, with a large roundabout where Uncle Harry took a right turn. The sign pointing straight read "Kyrenia Center," another pointing right read "Beylerbey" the name the Turks gave to the village of Bellapais. There was also a brown colored sign that read "Bellapais Abbey" pointing right.

They now continued on a road perpendicular to the shore, buildings rising left and right of the road, more stores with Turkish signs. Her aunt and uncle commented about how they didn't recognize the place, the villages they remembered from their young days living there had blended one with the other from development. The road then snaked up towards the mountains, becoming greener and more residential, with beautiful villas and condo developments on large plots of land.

The mountains loomed above, and Netta saw from the car window what she thought were ruins on some of the peaks of the rugged mountain range.

"Voufavento!" her aunt cried out pointing up above. "The one hundred and one Houses of Regina!"

"What is *that* Aunt Sophia?"

"Oh, those are Byzantine and then Frankish castles that were always part of the local legends. When we were kids, they would say that that's where Regina used to reside, who could be sometimes very kind and at other times, unbelievably cruel. She was the sovereign in medieval times."

"Saint Hilarion, on the right! Another castle, Netta," said her uncle.

"I want to hear more about the Regina, Aunt Sophia."

"And you will, when we sit down for a while, I'll tell you some of the stories." Sophia assured her. "Now, I want to focus on where we are, because we are almost at the village of Bellapais. Our time here is so limited, I want us to to see as much as we can."

The car suddenly came to a full stop just before a short bridge.

"Look," was all her uncle said pointing to the left. Netta's body was jolted by the image.

As if growing from the hillside, a building dominated the village surrounding it. Yes, this was what she had come to see, yet she hadn't expected such a visceral reaction to her first sight of the fabled Abbey. The car window framed a magical picture, and Netta understood that this view was one that had survived the ages. In her bones, she knew this was the same view her mother had seen, and her grandmother before her and a whole slew of ancestors going back many generations, before them.

Captivated by the sight of the Abbey of Bellapais, framed by tall cypress trees, Netta's eyes were fixed on it as the car drove over the bridge. The view to the left revealed the imposing Abbey's ruins majestically towering over the valley below that ranged all the way to the blue sea. Netta realized how high they were, and how beautiful the location of her mother's village truly was. The car now rolled down a narrower street with old buildings rising on either side of the road. They arrived at a small square.

Her heart was racing and her breath was caught in her throat. Nothing prepared Netta for the sight that rose to the left. The image from her mother's photograph was now there before her, no longer a one dimensional, faded relic of time, nor an image in the distance, but a massive stone edifice, garnished by towering cypresses rising to the sky.

As soon as the car wound around the perimeter of the Abbey and arrived at the parking lot facing the sea below it, Netta jumped out. Beyond her control and understanding, something propelled her towards this ancient relic. In her wildest dreams she never imagined she would have reacted like this. It was as if a cage opened, and she was spreading her wings and flying freely for the first time.

She ignored the few tourists walking the grounds with phones ready to click and walked towards a large stone doorframe. It was in the back of the Abbey and led to a large rectangular space. When she stepped through the threshold of the Abbey she was transported into another world, another dimension, and another time. Netta forgot about her relatives and began to explore the Abbey of her dreams.

She turned left and eyed the large room. It was missing its ceiling and the second story. Time had taken its toll, but a lot of the structure was still standing. The remains of two carved, marble thrones sat at the north side of the room and in the center was a Greek column that might have served as a table. Carved seating framed the west wall of the chamber, as if still waiting for its long-ago inhabitants to congregate and pay tribute to their high guests.

Netta was alone there. She walked towards those worn stone thrones, stood over them and ran her hand over their rough surface. Her head felt as if it was floating, and her body knew in every cell the stones and structures around her. She sat on one of the thrones and gazed around her. To the right, a longer chamber filled with rubble on either side, ended at a far wall with a round carved window facing the sea with a gated arched door. She looked up and saw that this part of the Abbey once spanned two high floors, because the west wall was still standing with eight arches, windows and what looked like cubby holes. The broken exposed part that was the floor showed the secrets of this building with myriads of stones packed together with mortar to create the ceiling of the first floor and the floor to the second.

As if in a trance, Netta walked through the door of that wall and into an arched Cloister. She looked ahead and at the end of the long colonnade she saw the arches of her childhood reveries flanked by the towering dark green cypress trees.

15 : Annie

JULY 1571

Annie had been watching the fight hidden behind some barrels, Marina a whimpering heap beside her.

Just as she realized that the pirates were storming their galley from all sides, a rough sack slipped over her head.

"John! Help," she cried. "Help me. Please, someone help me!" Rough hands grabbed her arms and legs and lifted her off her feet as she struggled to free herself.

"Put me down!" she demanded to no avail.

Nearby, she could hear swords whipping the air, clubs bashing bones, men's blood-curdling screams as they met some gruesome fate. Muffled sounds close to her signaled that Marina was probably suffering the same fate as she.

There was a strange feeling in knowing she would not be alone in whatever darkness lay ahead for her.

She was hoisted over someone's shoulder, her face against his back, his strong body odor assaulting her nostrils. Finally, she was deposited against a hard surface, Marina's cries next to her. They seemed to be in a small boat, she could hear the oars rising and falling into the sea. Her hand crept along the wood and found her maid's trembling hand and grasped it tight. Marina squeezed back, their joint plight uniting them.

The women were yanked to their feet and forced up a rope ladder onto the deck of a ship. They were led, still unable to see, along paths on the ship. They could hear men commenting on their appearance and feel hands reaching out to touch them before they were slapped away.

A door opened and they were both shoved in, and they could hear it being locked behind them.

Swiftly, Annie pulled the sack off her head and reached over to uncover Marina, who stood there, frozen. The two women embraced.

"Shush," she whispered in soothing tones to her maid, as if trying to calm a baby who woke up from a bad dream. When she finally felt Marina's body relax a bit, she let go and looked around.

They were in a well-appointed cabin, with thick rugs on the floor and a bed covered in expensive-looking textiles. There was a small velvet covered sofa at one end, and an ornately carved low table in front of it. Oil lamps were lit on the table and a side console, giving the dark room enough light so the women could see.

Touching the softness of the sofa, she thought that perhaps there would be civility in these pirates who abducted them. Ironic, she thought, because civility and piracy certainly did not go together. Yet, the fine coverings and furniture implied a discerning personality.

Perhaps in her misfortune, there might be a ray of hope.

Whoever the pirate was, perhaps she could appeal to his higher instincts and convince him to let her and her maid go without harm. Perhaps he could deposit them at some shore from where they could secure passage to Venice, their destination.

As she was contemplating all these possibilities, the door opened. A man entered carrying a tray with two bowls and a hunk of bread. The women recoiled, but it soon became clear that he was not interested in them. He deposited the tray on the low table and retreated, locking the door behind him.

16 : Netta

PRESENT TIME

Netta looked down at the length of the loggia of the southern flank of the Cloister of Bellapais Abbey. It was exactly the way she had imagined it to be.

She walked a hundred or so feet along the arched colonnade of ochre hued stone. Coming to the first of two sets of steps, she tried the wooden door at the top. It was closed. At the second set of steps, a metal gate lay open and Netta could see that it led to the church. *"I'll get there later,"* she promised herself and kept walking, eager to reach the arches of her dreams.

At the end of the colonnade, she stopped and there they were! Four stone arches, whatever remained of them after the many centuries since they were built. Four cypress trees soared above the ruins, creating a setting at once intriguing and stunning. This was exactly where her mother's picture was taken, and exactly where her own visions constantly transported her; a little girl giggling in a game of tag, chased by a boy she could barely glimpse as she turned to look.

Images of the children playing flooded her mind and she imagined that they were running around her, their voices, high pitched and loud, filling the air. It was almost as if she could reach out and grab one of them as they raced by screaming. Then, she was in the game herself, feeling the dew of the grass on her bare feet, the excitement of the chase on her hot cheeks. "*Tu ne peux pas m' attraper,* "You can't catch me," she shrieked in a language she didn't normally speak.

It was as if she and the Abbey merged in time; as if she, like an insect suspended in amber, was frozen where the past seeped in and melded with the present. Every cell in her body vibrated with the generational memories of her ancestors. The two worlds collided at that moment. A susurration from the tall cypresses swaying in the breeze tried to share an ancient truth.

Time fused in the here and the past, and Netta knew there had been someone else who'd lived here, in this ancient ruin, who played with the little boy in the Cloister. There had been a girl there. The girl of her visions.

"Netta!!" her aunt's voice beckoned her back.

"There you are! We lost you as soon as we arrived," she said.

"I've been exploring a little," she said, reluctantly shaking off the vision.

"Everything alright?" her aunt gave her a quizzical look.

"Yes, of course, why do you ask?" Netta stammered.

"You look sort of… I don't know," she laughed. "I thought we could go find your mother's house," she added seriously.

"Yes, my mother's house! Can I take a picture first, for mom?"

"Sure, I'll be waiting outside the gate."

Netta trained her iPhone to the shapes of the arches and snapped a few photos before she joined her aunt, uncle and Toula for a walk through the village to her mother's house. Her feelings were mixed. Even though her mother's house was important to her, she was drawn to stay longer at the Abbey. It had a magnetism that compelled her to stay.

They walked out into the square where a giant tree, the Tree of Idleness, her aunt had called it, dominated the area. Cafes were open around the square and touristy trinkets, cards and handicrafts were displayed outside some of the stores. The group skirted these and continued onto the narrow roads that led inside the medieval village. Her aunt and uncle held hands and kept stealing anguished glances at each other as they passed the houses that lined the sides of the street.

"Aunt Helen's house," her aunt whispered as they passed a low building with a small balcony entrance. "I used to come visit my cousins Irene and Chris here all the time." Her husband tightened his grip on his wife's hand.

They came to a crossroad and passed it to walk up the hill. They continued several feet before her aunt stopped in front of an arched entryway.

"Is this it, auntie?" Netta asked.

Her aunt nodded, clearly too emotional to speak.

"Can we go inside?" Netta said running her hand on the rough limestone wall that shielded the dwelling from the street.

"I don't know, my child," her aunt replied. "Unfortunately, we are at the mercy of the new occupants. Let's see if anyone is here."

"Hello, is anyone home…Hello…"

"Should we walk inside the courtyard?" Netta asked, taking a step forward.

Her uncle's hand stopped her before she entered.

"We don't want any trouble. Let's wait and see if anyone is here to let us in," he said.

Netta held back reluctantly. Here she was on the doorstep of her mother's childhood home, and she couldn't go in.

A female voice echoed from within in a language Netta didn't understand. A gray-haired woman emerged, whipping her hands on her apron. She stood sizing up her visitors.

"My mother's home," Netta said pointing inside.

The woman had a pained expression in her eyes. She nodded and gestured to them to enter. Her aunt almost ran inside, her footsteps guiding her into the familiar home. Netta felt as if she were in a trance. Was she really in the house her mother grew up in? Was there anything left of her mother's childhood here?

The woman kept a small distance from her unexpected guests and watched as Sophia exclaimed as she recognized familiar rooms and ran her hand over the old furniture. Netta, her cousin and her uncle exchanged glances. Sophia's heightened emotional state was palpable.

Netta followed her aunt and waited patiently for her to explain to her what it was she recognized. It was clear that this trip was as much, or even more, her aunt's journey down the painful paths of her childhood, as it was Netta's into her ancestry and the visions of the arched Abbey.

When they went once around the rooms surrounding the courtyard, her aunt's emotional turmoil seemed to settle a bit. She stood there for a moment, as if deciding what to do next. She grabbed Netta's hand, and she led her back through the rooms.

"This was where your mother's family cooked their meals, sat down to eat and rested around the hearth in the evenings." She pointed to the wide fireplace, filled with embers and ashes.

They then walked to the next room, "Your mother's room," she said. "We played here all the time. She had many dolls, and we'd sew them little dresses and have a fashion show. Right in here, in this very room." She ran her hand over the headboard of the neatly made bed. "This was her bed. I can't believe it's still here, after all these years. It's like a dream. I never thought I would see this ever again." She wiped her tears with her hand. "That was her dresser." Sophia walked over to the piece of furniture and caressed the top as if greeting an old friend. "She had the best clothes."

Netta was snapping photos as fast as she could. She wanted to be present and experience the place, but she also wanted to bring as much detail to her mom as she could.

And then she followed Sophia to the next room. "Her parents' room, may they rest in peace," Sophia crossed herself. "Your grandparents," she added. Netta walked around the home, feeling a connection and a new understanding of who her mother was. Grandparents, she'd had these grandparents who lived in this house! Those people were her ancestors.

Back outside in the courtyard, Sophia headed for a shed.

"This is where they kept their donkey to get around the village and to their fields and their goat for milk."

The old woman of the house was silent, and never seemed to lose her patience with the visitors. She watched carefully without intruding.

"We probably should get going," her uncle broke the spell.

"Do you want to go to your house, Sophia?" her husband asked.

"I can't bear to go there again. I went once. It's emotionally draining. I come, I see, and then I have to leave as if this wasn't where I grew up and where my ancestors are buried," she sighed.

Her uncle led Sophia towards the courtyard door, muttered a thank you to the old woman and walked out.

"I haven't been inside the church yet," Netta said as they walked back down the hill.

"Of course," her uncle replied. "We'll wait for you in the car."

They walked to the car; their bodies bent as if deflated.

Netta entered the Abbey grounds through the main gate this time. She walked towards the front of the church and stopped at the door, looking up at the fresco above the transom.

17 : Athanasios

AUGUST 1571

The air was thick with smoke; the battleground was burning. The remaining bedraggled soldiers of the garrison tied wet cloth over their faces and dragged their exhausted bodies to the bastions to defend the citadel.

Athanasios jumped ahead and crossed the yard towards the Ottoman invaders advancing over the breached wall. He wielded his sword above his head and let out a scream that tore his insides as he charged the men who filed into the city one after the other.

The first soldier, taken by surprise by the fierceness of the mad-eyed man, lost his head to the blow that Athanasios struck. But the men kept coming and Athanasios kept charging and striking and hitting and killing. Blood spurted from the wounds he dealt, and Athanasios found himself covered in it, his hand slipping on his sword hilt, his clothes sticking to him in the viscous fluid.

The battle raged on, and Athanasios lost track of how many men he had pierced with his sword, watching their last breath leave their astounded bodies, or how many he had beheaded, their arms still flailing as their heads flew off their shoulders. If one were to watch him from afar, they would have seen a madman, drowning in blood, drunk with it, massacring anything that jumped in front of him.

Finally, the breached wall was defended, and the Ottomans retreated. But for how long? The city of Famagusta had been under siege for nearly a year. The people inside were starving. They had eaten almost everything. Even the emaciated horses of the fighters had not been spared the knife of the hungry.

Marcantonio Bragadin called his officers and after much shouting and talking he asked to send an emissary to the Ottoman commander. With provisions almost gone, and gunpowder at its end, there was no choice but to salvage the civilian lives who were beseeching them to negotiate. They would negotiate terms of surrender.

Athanasios was spent. He'd only had a few pieces of bread and some well water in the past several days and his energy had waned. The last battle had taken everything he had to stay alive. The battle was won, but they were beaten. Without a way to get fresh supplies into the citadel, there was no energy left in any of them.

Word came back quickly that the terms of surrender were finalized and all Greeks were asked to leave the city. The Turks promised they would be unharmed. Athanasios walked around and found a Greek family ready to leave.

"Can you spare some pants and a shirt, sir?" He pleaded with the man." I will not be spared if I am found drenched in Ottoman blood."

The man looked at him in dread.

"You have killed many for your clothes to be soaked like that."

"I beg of you, don't let them kill me. Give me some clothes and I'll never forget it."

The man pointed to Athanasios' neck. He reached up and handled the gold pendant that Annie had draped around his neck.

"This?" he asked. "You want this for the clothes?"

The man nodded.

Athanasios sighed and took the pendant from his neck and handed it to the man.

The man instructed his wife to give Athanasios the clothes and hung the pendant around his neck.

Athanasios changed and discarded his ragged, bloodied clothes. The stone ring he had exchanged with his beloved for their wedding vows was the only thing of hers he now had left. He washed his face and hands as best he could and joined the Greeks who were leaving the fallen city.

18 : Netta

PRESENT TIME

The paved pedestrian street teemed with people, shops, cafes and restaurants. The buildings seemed frozen in a time before Netta was born, probably the fifties or the sixties, their limestone facades and filigreed iron window covers and railings in sharp contrast to the modern buildings she had seen outside the historic center.

Netta had returned from the visit to Bellapais Abbey, and she and her cousin were spending a little time in Old Nicosia, the divided Capital. Toula had ducked into an optical shop to pick up her mother's glasses while Netta stood outside people-watching. Clutches of young people around her age crowded the surrounding cafes drinking frothy frappes. One group of middle-aged women sipped their demitasse Greek coffees, nibbled on cookies, chatting idly, seeming to Netta as if they hadn't a care in the world. Yet, a hundred yards or so further down the street stood the outpost of the Green Line, the military demarcation point of the capital's separation splitting

Nicosia into two. To the North, a Turkish army sentry stood guard, in the middle, the Buffer Zone was occupied by the United Nations, and in the South was the Cyprus National Guard. Her cousin had already taken her to the demarcation line. Netta really didn't know how to feel at the sight of this blunt manifestation of the island's divide. She had snapped a few photos of the outpost, just like many tourists around her were doing, filing away the emotions until a later time when she could fully assess what this meant to her.

The past two days had been supercharged with emotions. The visit to Bellapais had brought her to the place of her lifelong visions. The visions had been the most powerful she'd ever experienced when she was on the grounds of the Abbey. Just when Netta thought she would clarify what they meant, the visit threw her into a maelstrom of more questions than she had before.

Yet, one thing had become clearer for her. Her mother's past. After the visit, Sophia sat down with Netta.

"It's time to talk about your mother," she said.

Netta sat silent, waiting for her aunt to continue.

"She was twelve, like me, when the Turks invaded," she paused. "No one expected the soldiers to reach our village that fast. We were scared."

Netta reached across the kitchen table and took her aunt's hand.

"My parents took me and my brother and we left early on, not waiting to see if the soldiers were nearby. Not so with your grandparents. They had decided to wait. They left with one of the last groups to flee the village." Sophia let out a long sigh.

"As they hiked over the mountain towards the east, they were ambushed by a group of Turkish soldiers. They were gunned down as they emerged through the pass. Your mother was discovered by the Red Cross under her mother's dead body. She had been there for two days, and she was in shock and near death. Your mother was the only survivor."

Netta gripped her aunt's hand.

"She was placed in a home for children without parents. We couldn't take her because we were living in a tent in a refugee camp. The Americans came and adopted her soon after. I think it was a good thing for her to be away from here. I don't know that she ever got over what happened to her."

The two women sat together without speaking for a long time. It had been a hard story for Netta to hear, but she needed to know exactly what had happened that gave her mother that permanent melancholic veil in her eyes.

"Go find Toula and go with her to pick up my glasses. Now that you've heard about the past, go live in the present."

And now she was here, in her mother's land, ready to discover more. The people milling about in Old Nicosia, where she waited for Toula, were a mix of locals doing some shopping and what she took for tourists. Some were women in headscarves speaking in, what she figured to be, Turkish.

A dark-haired woman in a ruffled, colorful dress and gold hoop earrings appeared before her unexpectedly. Her unwashed curls framed her face.

Her piercing eyes stared in a demanding way Netta could not turn away from.

Suddenly the woman grabbed Netta's hand and mumbled something Netta could not make out. It didn't sound like Greek.

The woman turned Netta's hand over and traced the lines of her palm with her index finger. An electric current ran through Netta's body. The woman looked up and fixed her dark eyes on her. Netta was entranced by her smoldering look. She made a half-hearted attempt to withdraw her hand, but the woman held on, and she, intrigued by this encounter, relented.

A palm reader, she thought. Why not?

There might be something she needed to know, now that she'd finally stepped onto the land of her ancestors.

At that moment, Toula stepped out of the shop and saw her cousin with the woman.

"Go away," she commanded. She attempted to remove the woman's hands from her cousin.

"Toula, no," Netta uttered. "It's okay, let her. In fact, I'm glad you're here. You can translate for me."

"She's a gypsy, Netta!" Toula exclaimed.

"Toula, let her, I want to hear what she has to say."

Toula resigned herself to the situation and took a step back from the gypsy woman.

Netta fully offered her palm to her and waited.

"*Asimose*," she demanded.

"She wants money. Give her a few euros," Toula said.

Netta fished a few coins from her pocket and placed it in the gypsy's hand.

A long pause followed, with the two girls watching expectantly as the gypsy studied the soft, tender palm of the young woman.

"You come from a far road," she finally uttered, her eye on the palm.

"We knew that." Toula piped in.

"Shush!" Netta said.

Toula gave her a side look.

"This road is longer than I have ever seen," the gypsy mumbled and traced a line in the girl's palm with her gnarled finger.

Toula rolled her eyes, but Netta gave her a "be patient" look.

"A church is where your road started, a big church," she continued. Toula quickly translated for Netta.

The two girls suddenly stopped fooling around and listened intently.

The gypsy continued tracing the girl's palm with a dirty finger.

"A man, I see a man, but you and he are separated by time, and a long sea."

Toula translated. The girls stood still, almost forgetting to breathe.

"*Ashkeri*, an army, battles, terrible times. You and he separated by the sea."

"A man..." Netta wondered.

"He not dead. He alive, not dead."

"What is she talking about?" Netta looked at Toula.

Toula translated but shook her head, "I dunno."

"He come for you, he come," the gypsy continued, her brow furrowed, her lips pursed. "The church, big arches," she went on.

"What about the arches?" Netta asked.

The gypsy looked up. Her eyes burned with a fervor Netta had not experienced before. She yanked Netta's hand and tapped her palm with her index finger.

"He come for you, like he promised."

The little hairs on the back of Netta's neck rose.

The gypsy's grip on her hand relaxed and she stepped away, disappearing into the crowd, as stealthily as she had appeared before her.

“Are you okay?”Toula shook her cousin.

“Yesss?” Netta stammered gazing at her palm.

“She’s just some crazy old gypsy, don’t read too much into what she said.”

“What about the arches?” Netta retorted.

“They all say that sort of thing.”

“What about being separated by sea?”

“She figured you’re a foreigner, so you must be separated by sea.”

“I see,” said Netta, still not able to shake off the eeriness of the encounter.

19 : Annie

JULY 1571

Annie had spent the night confined with Marina in the locked cabin. Despite her fear that the door would burst open any time and they would be dragged out to satisfy the desires of the pirates, she fell asleep exhausted, startled at every creak or sound on the deck.

In the morning, the same man brought another tray of food and swiftly locked the door behind him. The women had no chance to speak to him.

A lot of scurrying around could be heard on deck along with men's anguished voices and moaning and retching.

"Milady, I think there is disease onboard," said Marina.

"Something definitely is happening," said Annie.

She put her ear to the door. "I can hear men moaning and crying out. They are vomiting and I fear worse."

Suddenly the door was yanked open. Annie fell back on the floor and scrambled to escape to the far corner of the room. A man, wearing a navy-blue uniform with gleaming gold buttons, walked in. A dark felt hat covered his dark curls.

The two women cowered in the corner.

His blue eyes surveyed the women.

"We need nurses," he commanded.

"What's happening?" Annie dared to ask as she tried to peek outside the door.

"I'm Captain Uluj Ali. There's a blight ailing my men."

He grasped Annie's arm and pulled her outside. Annie blinked, momentarily blinded by the bright daylight.

The decks were soiled with vomit and a dozen or so men lay about holding their stomachs and moaning. The stench was unbearable, and she was grateful she hadn't eaten much, so her stomach was practically empty.

"Marina, get me my herbs."

She held her handkerchief to her nose and bent over one of the ailing men. She placed her hand on his forehead.

She looked at the captain.

"There's fever," she said.

Marina came back with the cloth medicine bag. Annie rifled through the contents and pulled out three sachets. Choosing fennel seeds for the stomach problems, and coriander and dried sage for the fever, she handed the bag back to Marina.

"We need boiling water," she looked up at the captain. "I'll make a medicine tea to help your men."

There wasn't much time to think of their plight during the next hours. She and her maid, assisted by the few men who were able to walk, boiled water and made large quantities of teas that were poured between the parched lips of the ailing pirates. The captain of the ship kept a close eye on the treatment of his men.

"Get someone to wash the decks," Annie took charge and gave orders to scrub the excrement and vomit from the soiled decks to keep the disease at bay.

Hours later, as her work was winding down, the decks were clean, and most of the men were now resting more comfortably, thoughts of her captivity reentered her mind. Annie stood by the bulkhead and took a good look around her. They were mid-sea. She didn't know where, with no land in sight. Yes, the pirates were mostly out of commission, but what could two defenseless women do to escape the terrible fate that loomed over them?

She leaned on the gunwale, looking out at sea and wiped her brow with her handkerchief.

"Thank you for all you and your maid have done for my men." The captain's deep voice startled her.

Annie turned around, quickly rolling down her sleeves, to cover her bare forearms.

"Sir, we had no choice in the matter," she replied. His eyes had taken on the dark blue of the Mediterranean Sea, and she noticed tinges of red at the ends of his unruly beard. Even as tired and unkempt as he was, she could see that he was a very handsome man.

"Forgive me, milady, for taking you and your maid from your ship, but we are pirates of these seas, and your vessel was sailing in our waters." A tired smile graced his mouth.

Annie stood there, not knowing how to respond. She was angry, she was tired, but she realized she was also grateful that their honor had so far not been disrespected.

"We did what we could for your men," she said. "And what do you intend to do with us, sir, may I ask?" she continued.

¤¤¤¤¤

Captain Uluj Ali had plied those waters for years, mercilessly seizing goods and people. He never wavered from his task to sell both to the highest bidder at the markets of Algiers. His reputation in the Mediterranean was fierce. He had mercy for no one.

Yet, watching this woman, obviously a noblewoman with her fine dress and her maid, treat his men with such dedication and care, had softened something inside him. He wasn't accustomed to being around female company of this kind. What he had known in recent years were the coarse women of the ports with whom he lain and satisfied his physical hunger. But, another hunger, the one of fine female company, had been harder to satisfy and even harder to admit needing.

Her youth added to his admiration, but it was her delicate beauty and direct gaze that entranced him. From the moment he opened that cabin door and laid eyes on her, he knew she was special. Through the treatment of his crew and the cleansing of the ship, he tried not to think about that. But now, he was completely captivated. Furthermore, he was utterly in her debt. And, as much of a pirate as he was, he was nothing without his honor.

Indeed, what would he do?

20 : Athanasios

AUGUST 1571

On that early August day, Athanasios followed the civilian population of Famagusta evacuating the city after its surrender. A Greek peasant had brought the Commander of Famagusta, Marcantonio Bragadin a platter bearing the severed head of Nicosia's defender, Nicolo Dandolo. It was accompanied by the demand by the Ottoman army of immediate surrender. Athanasios' horse had died of starvation during the siege, and the carcass had provided a much-needed stew for the troops. But it only lasted a few days. His fellow fighters, ragged and starving, had surrendered after the surrender agreement was struck.

But Athanasios didn't trust the Ottomans and decided to take his chances and escape unnoticed. Burrowed amongst other people, staying close to a family with three boys, he tried to blend in and pass as a Greek civilian.

Throngs of starving, scared people poured out of the burned gate of Famagusta, and Athanasios let the wave carry him out of town towards the countryside. The Ottomans were at the very moment searching for the fighters who'd defended Famagusta. He was certain they would be merciless with their *yatagan* swords when they found them. If he could pass as a Greek civilian, he hoped he would survive the terrible price his fellow fighters would pay.

Ottoman soldiers stood alongside the escaping people and searched the crowd for soldiers. He kept his head down and stuck close to the man and his family.

Outside the gate, Athanasios addressed the man.

"Where are you headed, my good man?"

The man drew his sons closer around him and did not respond.

"I have nowhere to go," Athanasios pressed on. "Can I come along with you?"

The wife tugged on her husband's sleeve and the family walked on, avoiding his gaze.

Athanasios knew that his survival depended on him finding a safe place to stay while he figured out what had happened in Bellapais. He stayed close to the family and followed in their direction.

Annie had been safely sent away to Venice, but his parents and everyone else he knew and loved were still at the Abbey. He had to make his way there somehow and find out what happened to them.

The family of Greeks arrived at the village of Acheritou late at night, Athanasios trailing not far behind them.

"All I need is a place to sleep," he tried to appeal to the man.

The father finally acknowledged him with a gaze and then they all walked towards a stone house on the outskirts of the village. The door opened furtively, and an older man hurriedly ushered them in. A nod from the man he'd followed, and Athanasios was let in.

A warm bowl of wheat berry soup was placed in the middle of a wooden table and each visitor got a spoon and a hunk of hard bread. Everyone dug in and Athanasios tried to eat less than his share so the children of the man who'd taken him in could have a little more sustenance on this, their first night of exile. Hardly any words were spoken. The old couple who took them in bit their lips and sat nearby watching the family eat what was probably their first meal in days.

Athanasios lay down to sleep on the cool dirt floor. The children lay closer to the door with their parents on either side keeping them close.

He woke up to the voice of the old woman and glimpsed the empty spot where the family had been sleeping only a few hours before.

"Leave us alone! Go away!" she shouted as Ottoman soldiers tried to shove her out of their way.

His arms were yanked from his sides and his body was dragged on the dirt floor and out through the door into the yard.

It was still dark, but he could make out the silhouettes of three soldiers.

The soldiers unleashed upon him all their fury for the eleven-month siege they had to endure. They kicked him in the sides, they punched him on his limbs, for what seemed like hours. Too weak to fight back, he lay there and prayed to God, as he was certain this would be his last day on earth.

He had no regrets for fighting against the Ottomans. As a warrior he knew from the start that he had put his life in the service of his country. The only thing that laid heavy on his breast was that he would miss a life he had always dreamed of with Annie. He'd only had part of a night with her as husband and wife and it was hard thinking he could miss the rest of their lives together. From the time he remembered himself and his life in the Abbey, she had been the light that brightened his days, the star he followed and the joy he pursued. As he grew into a man, he knew he loved her. At that beach, he had promised her that he would go back for her, but now, that promise hung in the night sky, between his beaten breast and his broken limbs. It lay in the warm blood that flowed from his wounds.

I wish you well, my beloved. Maybe in the afterlife I can fulfill my promise, but I hope for you, that won't be for a long time, was the last thought that went through his mind as a club met his skull.

The old lady and her husband had been cowering inside their small hut, the whacks and thumps of the beating reverberating in the night. The young man who'd sought refuge at their door didn't have the time to escape the Ottoman soldiers like the family he had followed there. She and her husband had aroused the father and his wife, whisking them and their children out the back door as soon as they'd noticed movement on the property. But after they gave the family a head start, there hadn't been enough time to rouse the young man who had been slumped exhausted on their floor.

Now they worried they would be next.

A terrible thump, rustling and then silence. That was their only clue that maybe the soldiers had left.

Georgia signaled her husband and walked towards the front room window. She peeked through the small opening she made by parting the tattered curtain and in the dark could discern a figure slumped in the front yard. Her eyes searched the area around the house. No one else was in sight.

"I'm going out," she whispered to her husband.

His hand shot up and he drew her close.

"Don't be foolish," he whispered in her ear.

She turned to face him, her wrinkled face grave.

"He could've been ours," she said, her hand covering her mouth.

Her husband put his arms around her.

"I know, I know. But we must be careful."

The old couple walked tentatively towards the door, opened it gently and stood at the threshold.

Once their eyes got used to the dark, they could see the young man collapsed in a bloody heap not far from the door. They looked around and cautiously advanced towards the figure.

Georgia knelt beside him and put her ear to his heart. She rose and nodded at her husband, Michaelis.

"He's alive."

The two old people grabbed him under the arms and dragged the unconscious man inside, all the while looking around for anyone lurking in the dark.

Once inside, they shut the front door and drew the curtains before lighting an oil lamp.

They surveyed the damage the soldiers had done to the poor man and began to undress him and, fetching fresh water from the well, clean and dress his wounds. His emaciated body had gashes on the arms and legs, and a few bones seemed to be protruding under the skin by his ribcage. Georgia gently traced the large purple bruises that had begun to form on his back, sides and legs as she tried to suppress a sob. Michaelis reached out and put a steadying arm on his wife's shoulders.

"We're doing our best, wife," he said softly.

A large wound on his head was bleeding profusely, and Georgia cut a piece of onion and placed it on the wound before wrapping a clean rag around his head as a bandage to keep it in place. A big swelling kept his right eye completely closed. They laid him down over a bed of straw and covered him with their meager spare bedding.

"That's all we can do for now, Georgia," Michaelis said and led his wife to bed.

Georgia was up before the rooster began to crow. The man was still and hadn't moved since they laid him there the night before. Kneeling before him, her gnarled hand touched his forehead almost in a caress.

"He's warm," she whispered.

Michaelis was up now too, and he stood by his wife. His brow was furrowed.

"What shall we do with him?"

"We'll try to bring him back, Michaelis," she said, stroking the young man's bandaged head.

"We'll have to be careful, Georgia. The soldiers might be back to finish him off."

"They thought they'd finished him off last night. Otherwise, why would they leave him?"

"You're right," he replied. "But still, we must be careful."

"What will we say if anyone sees him?"

"We'll say he's our son who got beaten up by bandits," he said.

21 : Athanasios

SEPTEMBER 1571

The young man walked into the yard, carrying an armful of wood from the fields.

"Good job, son." Georgia said as she greeted him by the door.

It had been a little over a month since he'd sought refuge there in the night and was dragged outside and left for dead by the Ottoman soldiers. His hosts had nursed him back to health, his bodily wounds healed. But Georgia wasn't so sure of his inner wounds.

As much as they tried, they couldn't find out anything about him. When he was unconscious, they'd searched his clothes and body for anything that might signify who he was. Nothing. All they found on him in his pocket was a stone ring tied to a red ribbon. They knew that he'd come from Famagusta, with the rest of the fleeing folks. They'd asked him where he hailed from, who his people were, but he always replied that he didn't know, he couldn't remember.

It was likely that the blow to his head had wiped away every memory he'd ever had. He didn't even know his own name.

They decided they'd call him Ioannis.

"Welcome Ioannis, my son." She smiled at the man. Truth was, that in his own misfortune, this young man had brought a light to the couple's lonely life in their old age. Their own son had been lost in the clashes with the Turks and they had no one. Life had been hard for them and after the young man regained his strength, having the extra help with the chores in the fields and the animals made a big difference.

That afternoon, as she sat in a low thatched chair by the door cleaning beans they had picked that day, she whispered to her husband who was taking a rest beside her.

"He needs a wife."

Michaelis looked at her saying nothing.

"He is young and there are plenty of young girls in the village that would be happy to have him."

Michaelis did not respond.

"He'll give us grandchildren, Michaelis," she said.

Michaelis nodded.

It wasn't long before Georgia had invited the matchmaker to her house. As they sat in the main room, facing the fields through the open door, the two women spun the yarn of matches for the young man.

"He's a hard worker, Marigo," Georgia said.

"Yes, but he was not well for a long time and Master Andreas might question that. He may be worried he can't provide him with grandchildren."

"Oh, Marigo!" Georgia laughed. "He's perfectly fine and see how strong he is, carrying all the wood from the fields, doing most of the chores around here."

She gave Marigo a long look.

"Besides, who do you think will be inheriting our property? Huh?"

Marigo paused.

"Oh, I hadn't known about that, but I see now that it makes him more of an eligible bachelor than before."

"We'll add a couple of rooms to the house and he and his wife will come live here. Whatever is ours, is his now. He's all we have."

Marigo nodded.

The two women finished their mint tea and candied fruit sweet. Marigo got up to leave. They parted with the understanding she was to procure a wife from the village for Ioannis.

22 : Annie

JULY 1571

The man who'd brutally attacked Annie's ship and abducted her and her maid was clear and unapologetic about who he was. He was proud to be in charge of a large fleet of brigantines plowing the East Mediterranean waters for pillage. Yet, there was something about this man that was not as coarse and savage as the pirates under his command that she'd encountered on board.

Captain Uluj Ali had addressed her politely and most importantly of all, he did not lay a hand on her or her maid, nor did he allow any one of his pirates to do such a thing. True, she and Marina had saved many of those savages' lives by using her herbal remedies and healing knowledge. But still, there was a certain aristocratic bearing to the man, portrayed in the fineness of his face and his erect posture and a certain kind of character evidenced by his personal treatment of his captives. Though she knew it was impossible, she hoped he would be a cultured man who'd spent time in drawing rooms, as well as overtaking ships at sea.

This assessment gave Annie an odd sense of hope. In the desperate situation that she and Marina found themselves, it was a thin shred of evidence that some goodness still existed in this man that prompted an expectation, perhaps, of mercy.

As she faced him on the deck of the pirate ship that had abducted her, she had a surge of courage. A lot depended on her answer.

"What would you like me to do with you, milady?"

Without hesitation she replied, "Release us, sir! Release us immediately!"

The young woman's courage and feistiness was a surprising change from the cowering women Uluj had first met in the ship's cabin.

He paused for a moment.

"And where would I release you?" he asked.

"I don't know where we are or how far from land this ship is. But I do know that we are a week away from Cyprus, and a day away from the shores of Candia."

The pirate's lips moved into the smallest, practically imperceptible smile.

"Smart girl," he exclaimed, almost despite himself.

He assessed the girl's dress; the silk betrayed its high quality through the stains from the bodily fluids of the sick. He observed her hair, wild and escaping the braids that were made perhaps days ago, her young face pale, showing the strain from hours of tending to his men. Her lips, pressed into a determined pout, tugged at his heart. She's just a child, he told himself to arrest the feelings that rose inside him.

"Well?" she demanded.

"As much as I would like to do that, it's not possible."

She gave him a questioning look.

"What would my reputation be if it were to become known that I had freed my captives instead of selling them at the slave markets of Algiers? How would I be able to plow these seas then? Where would the fear I instill be then?"

Annie's gaze did not waver from his as he spoke. She kept looking into his eyes, as if daring him to forget his pirate self for the moment and become the man, the human being he had once been. She dug deep for any kernel of humanity still left in him, any kernel of tenderness.

Uluj Ali shook his head as if to shake away the hold this woman had thrown over him.

"I'm going to get some rest," he said and gave a nod to one of his men before he turned on his heel and swiftly walked away.

Annie and Marina were escorted back to their cabin, the escort keeping a respectful distance.

"This is for your own protection, milady," the pirate softly said before he locked the door.

Marina collapsed on the couch and Annie laid her tired body on the bed. It wasn't long before her breath slowed to a soft rhythm and her mind began to float.

She was back with Athanasios behind the Abbey walls, feeling his solid body pressing into hers. As he leaned in to kiss her, she inhaled him and reached her hand to stroke his thick brown hair. She closed her eyes and leaned her head to meet his lips. His kiss was more ravaging than she remembered, rough almost violent in his tightening embrace. He bit her lips so hard that Annie opened her eyes.

She let out a scream.

"Wake up! Wake up, milady!" Marina was upon her, shaking her out of her nightmare.

Annie sat up on the bed trembling.

There was a knock on the door.

"Everything alright in there?" a pirate inquired.

"Yes! Everything is fine. Just a nightmare," Marina quickly replied.

Marina gathered her skirts and climbed up on the bed with Annie. She wrapped her arms around the shaken woman and rocked her gently.

"Hush, hush, it was only a nightmare," the young woman whispered.

As Annie's body began to relax, the women lay down on the bed together. After a while Annie spoke.

"It was horrible," she said.

Marina waited.

"I was back home. With Athanasios. He was holding me behind the wall, you know where we used to meet."

"Yes?" Marina said.

"He leaned in to kiss me,"The woman spoke as if in a trance.

"Yes…" the maid said.

"I closed my eyes and let him. He was rough and his hands were almost hurting me."

Marina sat up.

"He bit me! I opened my eyes…Oh Marina, it was horrible!" she dropped her face into her hands and started sobbing.

"I'm sorry, milady," she stroked the woman's hair. "It was just a dream. You know Athanasios would never behave like that."

"Oh, Marina, that's not the worst of it! I can't even say it. What I saw when I opened my eyes."

"Hush, hush now. You don't have to talk."

"It wasn't him! It wasn't him I'd been kissing. When I opened my eyes, that monster, the pirate was holding me in his grubby arms and kissing me!"

Marina sighed and laid back next to her lady. In the dark room, she put her body against the sobbing girl's and said nothing of her own fears and heartache. A salty tear ran down her cheek to her mouth, wetting the pillow beneath her.

¤¤¤¤¤

The seas were choppy when Annie woke. The feeling of dread that ruled her every waking moment returned immediately as she looked around her and saw that she was still in the cabin of the pirate ship.

She got out of bed and walked over to the porthole, parted the curtains and looked out to sea. There was no land in sight, none that she could see from her small vantage point, anyway.

She looked over to the couch where Marina was breathing heavily. The poor girl was sprawled on the sofa. Her arm dangling off the side, exhausted from the events of the day before, and the days before that. *What would I have done without her?* Annie thought as she watched the sleeping woman, merely a girl herself. *At least I'm not completely alone with these beasts, and whatever happens, I hope we are kept together*, Annie thought.

Suddenly, she heard the door unlock. She instinctively took a step back and gathered her dress around her.

The man from the day before stood in the threshold with two bowls of food and a hunk of bread. His demeanor was noticeably more respectful than the first day and he handed her the food and nodded before leaving.

She heard the door lock behind him and sighed. She placed the food on a table and walked over to the sleeping girl. Marina's face was slack, and her body conveyed the total surrender of the mind.

Annie stretched out her hand to shake Marina's shoulder, but she didn't have the heart to awaken her. Instead, she stroked her arm gently enough not to disturb her and sat on the floor next to her, reaching for her bowl of soup.

After a while, Marina's dangling arm began to stir, and Annie could hear her making moaning sounds.

"Leave us alone, I tell you!" Marina shouted to the intruder of her nightmare, her arms flailing to swat away the grubby male hands that surely were approaching.

Annie gently held the woman's wrists and softly tried to calm her down.

"Oh, milady, what are you doing?" Marina awakened.

"You're having a nightmare, Marina." She told her.

Marina sat up and leaned on the sofa. She looked around the cabin and sighed.

"The nightmare is still here, milady," she collapsed in her arms and sobbed.

23 : Athanasios/Ioannis

NOVEMBER 1571

Athanasios woke up at dawn and went to the well outside the little house he now called home. He drew up a pail of water, spilled some in an earthen bowl, and splashed some water on his face. Georgia and Michaelis, the two old folks who saved his life, had given him a roof over his head in their own home and treated him like a son. As much as he tried, he couldn't even tell them his own name. They gave him the name of their dead son, Ioannis.

He had gotten into the rhythm of the rural life, even though somewhere inside him he felt that it wasn't the life he'd once had.

He walked into the chicken coop and reached his hands into the straw to scoop out the still-warm eggs. He collected them into a basket so Georgia and Michaelis could sell them to women who came by the house looking for fresh eggs for their children. Then he went to the barn to milk the goats. The warm flesh of the animal in his hands gave him a certain comfort and, as he repeatedly squeezed for milk, his mind wandered.

He knew there had been a life before this. Yet, as much as he waded around the maze of his brain, searching for the place, the home, his people, his identity, he came upon forbidding walls of darkness. Everything began and stopped in this village where he dropped out of nowhere coming out of Famagusta, as Georgia and Michaelis told him.

Famagusta was now reported to be a desolate place. The news coming out of the town was that great carnage and brutality had followed the surrender of the Venetians. Michaelis told him that it had been recounted that Marcantonio Bragadin, the Venetian Commander charged with the defense of Famagusta, had been tricked by Lala Mustafa to surrender under the promise that everyone would be allowed to leave the city unmolested. Instead, he had been flayed alive. His skin was stuffed with straw, his military insignia attached, and he was paraded on an ox through the streets of Famagusta. Together with the severed heads of Generals Alvise Martinengo, Gianantonio Querini and Castellan Andrea, Bragadin was hoisted upon the masthead pennant of the personal galley of the Ottoman commander, Amir al-bahr Mustafa Pasha, to be brought to Constantinople as a trophy for Sultan Selim II.

Every Christian remaining in the besieged city had been slaughtered. Ioannis wondered whether his own family had perished in that massacre. Had he been the only one to survive? The tall black walls of his mind blocked him from seeing what he'd left behind.

Maybe it was a merciful thing, since no one survived the Ottomans. If he didn't remember them, perhaps he wouldn't mourn them. Yet, in the deepest recesses of his heart there was a painful place, well hidden, that manifested in the dark of night. A phantom pain throbbed when he lay alone on his straw bed, resting the weary body he tested by the back-breaking farm work.

He was certain that, though he couldn't remember, he had suffered a loss so profound that his mind failed to fathom it. He felt an absence so strong that if he allowed himself to open his mouth to scream, his scream would fill the entire village and reach all the way to Famagusta. There had to be someone he was longing for, but he might never know who.

"Good morning, son," Michaelis peeked into the barn. Ioannis figured the old man was over sixty.

"Good morning, Master Michaelis," Ioannis replied.

"Don't call me that," Michaelis replied. "Better to call me Father, in case the Ottomans come around asking about you."

"Aye," Ioannis said and nodded. The warm milk kept splashing into the pail as the animal strained against his hands.

"When you're done come inside the house. Georgia wants to speak with you." The old man turned to leave.

"Oh, and be sure to call her mother," he added as he walked away.

Ioannis finished the milking and brought the pail inside the three-room house. The middle room where he entered was dominated by a broad hearth, set with blackened pots on its stone rim. A weathered wooden table stood nearby with four wobbly thatched chairs. The two small squat chairs that the couple used when sitting by the fire at night, stood near the hearth. A stool had been added so he could join them.

He handed the pail to Georgia, and she motioned for him to take a seat. Michaelis stood close by.

She set the pail on the table.

"You have come to us unexpectedly during a difficult time for everyone."

He nodded.

"As you know, we had a boy, about same age as you," she continued. "We lost him during the raids. The Ottomans..." she wrapped her finger around the edge of her apron.

"I'm sorry for your boy," Ioannis bowed his head.

"If it is what you also want, we're asking you to settle here with us. It's not much what we have, but what we have is yours. We have no one else."

Ioannis lifted his head and looked from Georgia to Michaelis.

"The village has a lot of good girls. You are of marrying age, Ioanni." She let it sink in, her restless hands smoothing the fabric of her apron.

"You should think about taking a wife, having a family. How are we going to survive the Turks if we don't continue our blood lines?" she added bending closer.

Ioannis hadn't even thought much about a woman, let alone marriage since recovering from his injuries. He was a man lost; his body almost broken. How could he think of a future?

"What do you say, son?" Georgia said.

Ioannis took a moment before he answered.

"Who would want to marry a man who doesn't even know where he comes from? Doesn't know who he is?"

She grabbed his hand.

"There are plenty of girls in this village who would be lucky to have you."

"I have nothing, not even a name to give them."

Georgia and Michaelis exchanged a glance.

"That's not true, Ioanni." Michaelis spoke. "You have a family, right here. Us." He pointed to himself and his wife. "You have a name, Ioannis."

The young man sighed.

"And you have this property to house and raise your family." He added.

"What do you say son?"

Ioannis sat silently, staring down at Georgia's gnarled hand on his.

"I'll think about it." he finally said.

24 : Annie

1571

It had been several hours since Annie and the Captain parted ways, several hours since she'd asked him to set her and Marina free and he had demurred.

As she lay on the bed, her eyes closed, her mind raced thinking about their fate. Did the captain aim, as he said, to sell them as slaves? Who would be able to ransom them? The fate of her father was unknown to her at that time and moreover, she didn't know if Athanasios would come for her as he had promised. Those were the last words he had said to Annie, and she held them dear. Like the red ribbon that binds husband and wife at their wedding, she felt his promise reach through space and anchor him to her soul. He would come for her, she knew it.

If the Venetians had defeated the Ottomans and pushed them out to sea, her father and her beloved would probably be safe. But, if the unimaginable had happened, then she and Marina might be completely on their own.

Marina, who'd been with her since they were both children in the Abbey, was a fine maid. She was loyal and capable. But, Annie knew that Marina couldn't get them out of the dire circumstances they were in.

That task, she realized, would have to fall, entirely, on her. She had to save herself and Marina. She would have to keep them both safe until Athanasios came for her.

As exhausted as she was, Annie couldn't rest. She rose from the bed, careful not to wake Marina, whose fitful sleep came with difficulty. She picked up her medicine bag that was never far from her reach. Her fingers felt, through the fabric, the pouches of herbs and small bottles of potions. She stopped when she grasped that which she had been searching.

She lifted the tiny bottle out of its casing. In the semidarkness of the cabin, she held it to a small ray of light and gazed at it before slipping it into her bosom.

Tiptoeing back to bed, she closed her eyes and gripped the small vial through her dress.

She was sleeping deeply when a rough hand across her mouth startled her awake. She struggled to free herself, but the man who had hold of her had a good grip.

"The captain wants you," was all he said to her as he yanked her to her feet and out of the cabin.

The man opened a door on the ship and shoved her in.

"Leave us," she heard Uluj's voice in the dimly lit quarters.

The door shut behind her and she stood shivering.

Uluj was standing directly across from her. His naked broad torso gleamed in the flickering light of the candle. All he wore was a pair of breeches.

"I'm sorry to have woken you at this hour, milady," his tone was polite but under the surface there was a hidden coldness.

Annie stood silent, gathering herself and breathing deeply to steady her body and her soul. Being dragged in the middle of the night to the captain's quarters could only mean one thing.

Uluj took a few steps closer, then came to face her, so close that she could feel his hot, alcohol-laden breath.

He circled around her, as a hunter circles his prey. But this prey had already been snared in the trap and could no longer bolt. His male musk wove like a net around her, already invading her, already violating her.

Annie's body by that time had stopped shaking and her mind had gained full control. If what she feared was to happen, she decided that she needed to use it to her full advantage to stay alive.

Uluj ran the back of his hand across her face.

"I'm not going to hurt you," he whispered, his voice hoarse.

Annie did not react or reply.

"I've been thinking about you all night," he continued. "You've entrapped me with your beauty and I'm your slave."

Annie kept her gaze ahead. He took her hand and guided her to his bed. She complied, like an automaton, putting one foot in front of the other, as if she was walking through a viscous body of liquid. She'd feared this moment since they were abducted from their ship. She aimed to survive it. Athanasios made her a promise, and she wouldn't let him down.

Uluj sat her at the edge of the bed. He stood back a moment and looked at her, his gaze piercing the most private places of her being, He reached out his muscular arm and gently pushed her back on the bed. He climbed up next to her and reached for her body. Annie closed her eyes, as his hand wandered all over her, so she wouldn't have to look at her assailant. Time slowed down and Annie's breathing was barely audible. When she felt him pull up her dress, remove her undergarments and violate her, she felt her mind leave the confines of the cabin and fly over the fields and orchards of the Vasiliki, across the arches of the Abbey, where she felt herself running barefoot in the early morning dew.

When it was over and Uluj rolled off her and turned his back to sleep, Annie gathered her clothing and crept to the far side of the bed, crouched in the fetal position. That was when she finally allowed her tears to flow, silently, while Uluj snored beside her. She clutched the small vial that she had hidden in her bosom that, miraculously, Uluj had not found in his rush to ravage her. She had not had the opportunity to do anything with it before the rape. But she still had it, and that was a lot.

The next morning, she felt Uluj rise early and get dressed. Annie pretended to sleep.

He leaned over her, and she opened her eyes.

"You will stay with me from now on," he instructed her.

Annie stifled a cry. She steeled herself and heard herself speak.

"What of my maid?" she asked.

"Your maid?" he said.

"Yes, the girl that was with me, I cannot be without my maid."

"She probably has a man of her own now," he said slyly.

Annie cringed thinking about Marina's fate at the hands of one or more of the pirates. She tried not to show her feelings of revulsion.

"But I can't be without my maid," she insisted.

Uluj paused for a moment. He came closer to the bed and sat down beside her. He stroked her arm, and she tried hard not to pull away.

"I will instruct my man to bring her to you. She can live here with you during the day. At night, she'll have to return to her own quarters."

Annie's heart broke into a million pieces. This meant that both she and Marina were to be ravaged over and over by these beasts. How would they be able to bear it, she wondered?

Shortly after he left, the door opened, and Marina was shoved inside before the door was locked once more.

The girl was a heap on the cabin floor, her body shaking, and her hair in disarray. Her face was bruised and swollen, and her clothes, torn and bloodied.

Annie put her arms around the girl who had been her companion all her life. Marina let out a cry as if an animal were inside her and was fighting to get out. Annie held her tight and talked to her soothingly, trying to help the poor girl release the fear and the pain that she'd suffered at the hands of the savages.

"Marina, I'm here now. Marina dear, I'm here. You're with me now. You're safe," she kept saying.

As she held on to the girl, Annie acknowledged that their ordeal was not over, and they'd have to steel themselves for the days to come, until they were rescued.

Was the Captain still planning to sell them after he had satisfied himself? Marina was in no shape to discuss the fears that were going through Annie's head. For the first time in her life, Annie had to make decisions all on her own. Growing up, Grandmother made decisions for her. Once she passed away, Father took over. Even the decision to become betrothed to Athanasios had not been hers, even though in the end, her father's desires had aligned with hers. The decisions facing her now, were not just any decisions, but decisions of life and death.

As the girl's shaking subsided to a subtle quiver, Annie led her to the couch in the captain's quarters. She didn't have to ask Marina what had happened, she knew all too well. She regretted not discussing the possibility with her before this happened. Maybe if she had advised Marina not to fight, she would have fared better. Annie herself had made those decisions as the events had unfolded. Survival is a very strong instinct, and as much as she had wanted to fight for her honor, she very well realized that it would leave her not just raped but also possibly dead. Annie had too much to live for. She wasn't going to relinquish her life without trying to reunite with Athanasios.

The time on board the pirate ship now proceeded with the women spending time together in the captain's quarters during the day, and in the beds of the men who took their bodies at night. Annie had long talks with Marina. She advised her to persevere. They talked about what had happened to them, they cried, they cursed their fate, but Annie made sure they did not despair.

"How are we ever going to be rescued, milady? Does anyone even know where we are?" asked the beleaguered girl.

"We are in a tough place, Marina. But we are not going to despair. Athanasios and Father are surely looking for us."

"Are they even alive?" the woman blurted before she capped her mouth with her hand.

Hearing the thoughts spoken aloud felt like a blow to Annie's entire being. She took a moment before speaking.

"We don't know anything. If John has been killed or captured by the pirates, there is no one left to know our fate."

Marina nodded in agreement.

"What are we going to do, milady? I don't know how much more of this I can take." Her big brown eyes implored Annie. "Sometimes I feel like hauling myself overboard and ending this ordeal."

"Oh, Marina! Please don't talk like that. And what will I do alone? I need you. We need each other."

Marina lowered her head and began to cry.

"Shush. We don't want them to hear us crying. We need to be strong."

She embraced the crying girl and rocked her in her arms.

"I have a plan," she whispered in her ear as she held her tight.

Marina's body stiffened.

"What plan?" she whispered back fighting a sob.

"We must get off this ship. We must convince the captain we are not going to run away and talk him into allowing us to get off the ship at his next destination."

"Where do you think that will be?"

"I don't know, but he has to dock somewhere for provisions, don't you think?"

Marina had stopped crying and paid attention. The two women talked, their voices mere whispers until night parted them.

The next morning, after another night of horror for the young women, the captain left the cabin early. Marina was brought in a little while after.

As they were settling in for their day together, the sounds of rushing feet out on deck told them something was afoot. Whooshes like sails furling could be heard, men calling at each other, making haste to accomplish something.

Annie's heart began to thump. She grabbed Marina's wrist.

"This is it! This may be what we've been waiting for," she excitedly said to her.

Marina stood still. Tears began to run down her cheeks, and she tried to wipe them with her free hand.

"I can't believe it, milady."

"I think we're near land. We're preparing to anchor."

The two women ran to the porthole. Annie thought she saw land in the distance. It felt as if the cabin she was confined in had expanded, dropped its walls and unfurled a bridge that might lead them to freedom.

Her fingers dug deep into Marina's arm.

"Look. Look carefully in the distance," she said, her voice throaty.

Marina pulled Annie's clawing hand from her and leaned in to peer through the porthole. She remained still for a long while, looking. The two women embraced and stood there for a long time.

When their tears were finally spent, they sat by the side of the bed whispering and waiting.

25 : Athanasios/Ioannis

1572

Ioannis had been taken aback by the discussion he'd had with Georgia and Michaelis. A little over a month ago, they told him that, after the destruction of the city of Famagusta, there would be no way to find his family. Besides, it could be dangerous for him to begin asking questions. He was better off keeping to a quiet life. They had also suggested that he was of marrying age.

It was one thing to be asked to call them Mother and Father and another to be told to take a wife.

After the initial shock, and after mulling it over in his head a while, he began to accept that it made a lot of sense.

However, there was nothing he could say to them that could explain how he felt.

The thought of taking a wife somehow threw him into a panic. He understood very well that the customs were such that marriages were arranged. It was the proper way of doing things. Girls were kept inside, protected from male gazes and only allowed to meet with a man after they were betrothed. Yet, to him it seemed so unnatural.

A couple of months had passed by since the people who had rescued him told him he would be their heir. Anyone else in his place might have welcomed the offer to start a family and raise it on the homestead. A nagging feeling, though, kept Ioannis from seriously considering it.

Under the watchful eyes of his new parents, Ioannis kept to his daily routine. He felt their quizzical gaze when he bent down his lean frame to gather the eggs, when he took off for the fields to tend to the olive trees, when he walked down to the citrus orchards, when he fed the animals.

After sunset, sitting around the hearth once supper was done, the embers barely glowing, the three of them would barely break the stillness.

"That goat needs more fresh air," Georgia said.

"Aye, and the chicken coop needs some cleaning, I think," the old man added.

"I'll be sure to get to it tomorrow," Ioannis replied respectfully.

The old people tip toed around Ioannis, not really knowing what he was thinking. The silence hung like a smokescreen between them.

"Georgia, you shouldn't have pushed him so quickly. He's not ready." Michaelis would whisper at night, when the couple was alone in their room off to the side of the kitchen.

"I thought he would be happy to take a wife. I thought it would change his sullen mood to have a woman in his bed, maybe a child on his knee."

Michaelis turned to his side.

"All I know is that since we spoke to him about it, he's been more closed-up than usual."

Georgia sighed.

"Do you think he will leave us?"

"I sure hope not. I've become fond of him, and even though he can never take the place of our own son, he is a good boy, respectful and a hard worker."

"What would we do without him?" Georgia said biting her lip.

"There's no need to press him now. Let's wait until he decides on his own."

Georgia now cried softly.

"I just wanted some grandchildren running around my yard. Is that so much to ask after we've lost so much?"

Michaelis turned and put an arm around his wife.

"No, it's not too much to ask. Be patient. He'll come around."

He kissed her wrinkled cheek softly.

"Go to sleep now. We've got a lot to do in the morning."

The next morning, Michaelis and Georgia made an extra effort to be kind.

After their breakfast of stale bread softened in water, raw onion and a handful of black olives, Michaelis walked with Ioannis towards the animal shed.

"Tomorrow is Sunday, son."

"Yes," Ioannis replied.

"Georgia washed and dried your clothes. How about you come to the public house with me after church?"

The village they lived in had a small square where two storefronts stood across from each other. The owners would put a few thatched chairs outside in the sun and a boy would carry trays laden with glasses of sweet mint tea.

The village men spent their late afternoons and Sundays after church meeting in the public houses in their square. They would sip their mint infusions while sitting with relatives, neighbors or associates. Sometimes, if there was a little extra money, they would order a *zivania*, the Cyprus pomace brandy, distilled from the fermented remains of wine grapes.

As the days after his rescue lengthened into weeks and months, Ioannis had begun to become a little more interested in the world around him. The solitude of the farm had helped in his healing. As his physical wounds had mended, he welcomed the activity of the outside world.

"Aye Father," Ioannis replied. "I will come."

Later that day, he and Michaelis, dressed in their clean Sunday clothes, rode the mule the two miles into the village square. They tied her to a tree nearby and walked over to two unoccupied chairs set apart from the other patrons.

They sat next to each other, facing the square and the church.

The public house owner ran out and they ordered two sweet mint teas.

Around them there were several groups of men, some alone and some together, sipping tea, chatting or just sitting quietly. By now, most everyone in the village had learned that a young man was living with the old couple who had claimed he was their son.

Some of the men began to whisper to each other as Michaelis and Ioannis sat down.

"There's Michaelis and his son. But how can this boy be from here? Their son was dark as a crow and his hair curly and black."

"Yes," the other man in the high boots replied. "He looks nothing like him. This Ioannis is light skinned and has hair made of wheat. His body is tall and lean, not like the shorter, squat bodies of the men in our village."

"Yup, doesn't look like he was used to too much farm work growing up."The other man whispered.

Michaelis and Ioannis tried to ignore the looks and sat gazing out at the church.

In contrast to the dark skinned, brown-haired boy who grew up in their village, it was true, Ioannis had light hair and green eyes and he was tall. It didn't escape anyone that there was something almost regal about the way he carried himself.

The server boy arrived with their drinks and deposited a small tray with the glasses on a nearby chair. The two men sipped their tea silently and watched the people passing through.

"I'm glad you came out with me, son," said Michaelis.

Ioannis looked at the man whom he now called Father.

"I don't know who your people are and exactly where you come from, but Georgia…Mother and I are happy to have you here with us," he continued.

Ioannis nodded.

"I'm grateful to you both," he finally said, his eyes clear with sincerity.

The tea emanated its strong aroma and the men continued to take small sips, savoring the refreshing flavor. Michaelis turned to his son and noticed his gaze distracted by something in the side street. He followed his son's eye to land on a young girl, walking beside an older woman, each carrying earthen urns of water on their shoulders. The young woman's right hand held the urn aloft, and her left bent at her slender waist, braced her lean body for the weight of the water.

"Hmm," he softly remarked.

Ioannis, as if his trance was broken, turned to look at his father.

"What?" he inquired.

An idea of a smile formed on Michaelis' weathered face.

"Nothing," he replied shaking his head.

After they'd finished their tea, Michaelis called the boy over.

"Two *zivanias*, young man," he ordered. It was a splurge to order the fragrant spirit, but he felt that with Ioannis at his side on that day, he did have reason to celebrate.

The drinks were served, and he and his son lifted the shot glasses of strong spirit to their mouths, sipping in silence.

The next few days passed in the now familiar routine of the daily chores of the farm. Michaelis didn't mention anything about the girl on the street to his wife, not wanting to create expectations. But he felt a growing germ of promise for a renewed future for all of them.

A week later, when Ioannis entered the small kitchen holding the egg basket, his hands faltered and almost dropped the eggs. A young woman, with alabaster skin, pink lips and a stray strand of curl escaping the bounds of her scarf was standing there. She was flanked by Georgia and an older woman.

He immediately recognized her as the girl he'd noticed at the square on the Sunday outing with Michaelis.

"Oh, there you are!" Georgia exclaimed taking the basket out of his hands.

The girl turned and lifted her dark brown eyes to him. His stomach tightened.

Georgia looked at the two young people for a long moment.

"This is my son, Ioannis," she said to the women. "He's such a help to us, doing so many chores."

The older woman nodded her head.

"Pleased to meet you," she said.

The young woman nodded and lowered her eyes, her long lashes sweeping down her cheeks.

"Pleased to meet you," she murmured and retreated closer to her mother.

"Ioannis, let me introduce you to Penelope, and her mother Andriana," Georgia said. "They were just asking for eggs. So glad that you brought them on time."

"My pleasure," Ioannis said taking a small bow and finding himself taking a step towards the women.

"I was just ready to make a cup of tea for me and Ioannis." Georgia said.

Ioannis gave her a quizzical look.

"We always take a mid-morning tea break," she continued staring at Ioannis. "We wake up so early to tend to the animals."

"Why don't you join us?" she continued.

The invitation was hard to turn down. Ioannis was moved by this young woman whose innocent beauty had caught his attention. But somehow, he had this gnawing feeling that he was doing something wrong.

"I still have to weed around the orange trees," he heard himself saying.

Georgia looked at him sternly.

"Surely the weeding can wait a few more minutes, while you have a cup of tea with me and our guests?"

"I'm sorry, I can't stay," he said to the guests, and then he turned around and headed out the door.

26 : Netta and Thanos

PRESENT TIME

Netta planned to meet with Thanos for a frappe that afternoon. He had texted her the night before and told her where to meet him. Toula was curious and thought maybe she and Fivos should go with her, but Netta put an end to that.

"No, Toula," she said. "I need to meet him on my own. I'll be fine. He's just a man."

Toula relented.

"Okay then. Fivos and I can drop you off."

After Auntie's generous lunch and a proper Cyprus siesta, Netta rose to get ready for her rendezvous. Her suitcase didn't offer much choice in clothes, but she rummaged through and pulled out a fresh pair of jeans and a form fitting white tank top. For jewelry she slipped on her fun plastic flower ring and her dangle earrings. The mirror showed a slender, nice looking young woman and she turned to pick up her bag to go. Draping it over her shoulder, she signaled to Toula that she was ready.

The three young people got in the car, Fivos at the wheel, and drove towards the Island Café.

"So, what's happening with you two?" Fivos asked.

"Ach, awkward!" Toula piped in.

"Why awkward?" He persisted. "Is it bad that I want to know what my cousin is up to?"

"Yes!" both girls retorted.

"Besides," he continued, "I think I could give you some good advice. After all, I've known Thanos for a long time."

"We're just going to talk about Bellapais." Netta said.

"Oh, talk about Bellapais! How exciting!" mocked Fivos. Toula gave him a small swat on the shoulder.

"Let her be, Fivo. Just because you don't have anyone interested in you right now..."

Netta tried to ignore them. The anticipation of seeing Thanos again was overwhelming, and the closer she got to the café, the more excited she became.

"Here we are." Fivos parked the car at the curb and let her out. "Call me when you want me to pick you up."

"Okay, bye," she gave a small wave and walked away.

She went up the few steps to the entrance and stopped at the door to scan the near empty tables for Thanos.

Her heart made a summersault when she spotted him. From his broad smile, she could see he was happy to see her. "*What is it about this man?*" she thought as she neared.

Thanos got up and gave her a small peck on the check. He pulled out a chair and let her sit before he joined her. She threw her bag on the chair next to her. The aroma of strong Greek coffee was intoxicating, and much welcome in the hot afternoon doldrums.

"I'll have a Greek coffee," she ordered when the waiter came around. Thanos gave her an approving look and ordered one for himself.

"And I'll have a chocolate cake, please," she added, wanting to finally try the awesome looking desserts behind the glass displays.

They settled back in their chairs, happy to be with each other alone and yet, not knowing where to start.

"I..., "Thanos started talking while at the same time Netta opened her mouth to speak.

They both laughed.

"You go first," he said.

"No, no, you go," she insisted still giggling.

"I wanted to say I'm happy you came."

"Me too. It's nice to be here," she said looking into his eyes.

"So, you went to Bellapais?" he asked.

She nodded.

"How was it?"

Netta took a moment to gather her thoughts before she answered. She had not told him about her visions. Could she tell him that while she was in Bellapais it felt as if she were in a time vortex, powerful enough to swallow her; could she tell him about the little girl and the little boy?

"It was amazing," she said.

"How so?"

"I don't know if I've told you this, but ever since I was a little girl I was fascinated by a picture of my mother as a young girl by the Gothic arches," she said.

"Did you find the arches? How was it?"

"After all these years of imagining what that place would be like, I finally got to be there. And it was as magical as I always thought it would be."

Thanos listened with his eyes focused on her, as if he didn't want to let even one word, one syllable escape him.

"Bellapais is a magical place. And, of course, you can see from the Abbey that it has a long history. It's been sacked by the Genovese, the Venetians and the Ottomans. Not to mention, it's currently under Turkish occupation. It's almost as if history tends to repeat itself, but in this case, not in a good way."

The two young people moved their chairs closer and spoke leaning into each other, their heads almost touching. Their bodies conveyed an easy comfort; their limbs relaxed; their faces earnest, without a trace of self-consciousness. A passerby might have thought they'd known each other forever.

The coffee was served, and the chocolate cake sat between them with two forks. Without even a thought, they each dug into the cake, so familiar with each other, they ate from the same plate.

"I have a strange reaction to Bellapais, actually to the entire island," Netta said between sips of her coffee.

Thanos looked at her, his fork in mid-air.

"How so?"

"I'm not sure how to explain this without sounding a little, you know, woo woo."

"Try me," he said.

"It's as if I've been here before. As soon as I landed and that dry heat of Cyprus hit my face, it felt as familiar as the New York skyscrapers. Maybe even more," she paused. "Weird, isn't it?"

Thanos put his fork down and sat back in his chair. He folded his hands on the table.

"I wouldn't think so," he finally said.

"You don't?"

"Nope, it's perfectly not weird with me," he smiled.

Netta smiled back and picked up her coffee cup. She sipped the last drops, trying to avoid the muddy grounds at the bottom unsuccessfully. The gritty coffee grounds stuck around her mouth, and she reached for her bag to get a tissue.

He offered her a napkin and they both laughed easily.

"It's not weird to me that you said that about Bellapais. You want to know why?"

She nodded.

"I felt exactly the same way."

"Really?" she said. "Amazing. Do you think Bellapais is one of those places they talk about, a spiritual vortex with swirling centers of energy? A place like Sedona?"

Thanos looked at her.

"Sedona?" he asked.

"It's a city in the mountains of Arizona. It's become really famous for this."

"What? Seriously?"

"Yeah, there are places in the world where massive energies are concentrated. They say that a vortex can act as a portal for spirits travelling between two worlds."

He looked puzzled.

"Well, that's a bit, how did you say, woo woo," he said.

"Oh, now you're turning on me!" She cocked her head mockingly.

"No, I'm not, but I've never heard of such a thing before. I've never even considered it."

She continued to look at him. He was the first person to acknowledge even a sliver of the unusual things that she'd experienced. Could she tell him about the visions she'd had all her life, about the visions of Bellapais with the little girl and little boy playing in the Cloister? As much as she wanted to, it just didn't feel like the right time. They'd only known each other for such a short while, and it was really a bit "woo woo". Besides, she'd kept her visions to herself for so long that she didn't even know if she could share them with anyone, even if that person was Thanos.

They sat back and ordered more coffees to while away the afternoon.

"Maybe we ought to go to Bellapais together," he said.

"Yes, maybe we should." Netta replied.

27 : Annie

1571

A couple of hours had passed since Annie and Marina first glimpsed land. When they heard the rattling of the anchor chain dropping to the bottom of the sea, they jumped to the porthole. The sliver of land seen earlier afar, had materialized into the definite sight of a port city on the shore of a country unknown.

Annie tightened her hand on Marina, and they waited for the next move. Had they arrived in Algiers where the infamous slave markets flourished? Or, had they anchored at a European port, perhaps a midway stop for provisioning and giving the men some shore leave?

Neither woman knew what the orient looked like nor what Europe's shores might be like at all. They crammed their faces into the porthole trying to discern from the buildings in port where they were.

As the hustle above was continuing, they watched as boats were lowered into the water, ladders were thrown over the side and men boarded the boats and began to row ashore. Soon, the women realized that time was precious. They needed to be ready if they were called to disembark, as they hoped they would be.

"Bring me my medicine bag," Annie said.

"It's right here, milady," Marina handed it over.

Annie rummaged through the bag and took out a tiny bottle, identical to the one she'd had stashed on her person. She pulled Marina to her and tucked the vial in her bosom.

"Aye", Marina patted her breast as if she were touching something precious.

"We'll probably be separated tonight," Annie said.

"Aye," Marina responded. "It has to be tonight."

"Once the deed is done, we'll sneak out and meet each other wherever we can. Then, we'll figure our next step."

Marina nodded again; her brow furrowed. They quickly gathered up their few belongings in a cloth, wiped their faces with a wet rag and tried to smooth their braids as best they could. A pirate ship was a tough place for a woman, and there was little opportunity for washing with fresh water. Despite their circumstances, they were excited to be going on shore. Annie was ready to feel land under her two feet.

They didn't have to wait long, after the commotion died down, for their cabin door to fly open.

"The captain says to get ready for shore," an excited sailor announced.

"Where are we?" Annie asked as they followed the sailor out of the cabin.

"Genoa!" the sailor exclaimed.

Both women took a sigh of relief. At least it wasn't Algiers. The Republic of Genoa was an independent state on the Ligurian coast. It was one of the main commercial powers of the Mediterranean, one of the major financial centers in Europe.

A tender waited under the rope ladder they descended. The captain and his first mate were already aboard and helped the two women. As soon as they were seated on the plank benches, the oarsman began to row towards the port.

The spires of the churches rose into the clear sky above. Annie had never seen such a magnificent sight. Bellapais had been her only experience, and as beautiful and imposing as the Abbey was, it could not compare with the splendor of Genoa. The city's towers and bridges, visible as miniatures from a distance, came increasingly into relief as they approached the shore. For a moment, breathing the salty air and with the light breeze on her face, she almost forgot her predicament and let herself marvel at the splendor of the city.

It wasn't long before the boat deposited its passengers on the city dock. Annie looked to Uluj, trying to decipher his intentions. Did he mean to sell them, here, in Genoa? Was he looking for ransom or was he just planning to keep them as his own slaves? All of this was unknown to her, as much as she had tried to pry answers from him over the days of her imprisonment. Uluj kept his plans very secret. He hadn't even told her that they were anchoring in Genoa.

She and Marina were silent as they followed him and his first mate along the pier. Annie had never seen so much activity in one place. On the port side, baskets of goods were covered in a sturdy looking blue cloth she'd never seen before. She marveled at the buildings by the harbor, with their tall arched stone facades. Workers carried sacks of goods onto and off of ships and into and out of buildings. Bosses yelled and gave orders in a language she did not know. Pungent odors of animal dung, stale waters, and just plain old human sweat assaulted her nostrils. She pressed her handkerchief to her nose, trying to protect herself from the fetid port mélange.

Walking in her delicate shoes was hard, trying to avoid the rubbish of rotten fruit, horse dung and the sweaty bodies strewn on the thoroughfare, as well as trying to regain her balance from being at sea for two weeks. The sights and sounds were so new and interesting that Annie still tried to look around. The massive lighthouse, the Lanterna Uluj pointed out, sat at the mouth of the port, its sturdy spiral one of the tallest buildings she had ever seen. The crest of the red cross, captured in a gold circle, topped with a crown was easily visible, even from the distance where she and her group had disembarked.

Uluj reached over and took Annie by the elbow, helping to guide her through the busy port.

Soon they turned off the main road and onto a narrow alleyway, with tall buildings rising on either side, to the point that only a sliver of sky was visible. They walked along many such crooked streets, Uluj clearly walking with purpose, and after a few hundred yards, they stopped in front of an inn. Annie sought Marina's eyes, nodded and brought her hand to her breast. Marina gave an imperceptible nod.

They were all soon inside the inn. A portly man, whom Annie took to be the proprietor, rushed towards them and grabbed Uluj's hand in a vigorous shake.

"So good to see you again, sir!" he exclaimed. Taking him by the arm, he led them to a table.

"I'll have your rooms ready by the time you finish your supper," he said, needing no instructions from his customer. He motioned a waiter over and scurried away.

The tavern on the ground floor bustled with customers and the smell of cooked food soon made her realize how hungry she was for something decent to eat. All they'd had on board was a slop of fermented wheat that passed for food. Soon, platters of roasted meats glistening with melted fat, roasted vegetables and jugs of wine were placed on their table. A bowl of oranges followed.

Despite the uncertainty of their future, the two captive women dug into their meals with relish. They enjoyed the meats, savored the fresh bread, and quenched their thirst with red wine.

Annie managed to steal looks around the tavern between bites of food, noting the back door behind the long bar. A staircase led to a second story where Annie presumed the rooms would be situated.

The men ate hungrily, meat juices running down their beards, all the while keeping an eye on the women. They drank with abandon, and Uluj ordered a second carafe of wine. The meal was coming to an end and Uluj motioned for the tavern keeper to come close.

"Hot water for baths in our rooms," he ordered. The innkeeper gave him a look. Baths were frowned upon but men who had been out at sea a long time always asked for them.

When there was no more food left, Uluj rose from the table and led the way up the stairs and to the rooms he had reserved.

Once he ushered Annie inside, Uluj closed the door behind him.

In the center, steam rose from a tin bathtub. A bed, big enough to roll in and covered with clean, white bed sheets, was set against the wall. All Annie could think about was soaking her grimy body in the tub and then resting on the bed. But she knew that that wasn't what Uluj had in mind.

"Go ahead," he said, sitting on the only chair. "You go in first." He motioned towards the tub.

Annie didn't hesitate to strip her clothes and lower her weary body into the hot water.

"Ahh," she sighed as the warmth seeped into her bones.

The stress melted off her. Being Uluj's captive didn't stop her from enjoying that small little pleasure.

"Nice," he said as he moved to the side of the bed, watching her. Uluj had grown fond of her. She could tell that it wasn't only the sex, but that he'd become accustomed to telling her about his travels, asking her about her life. His feelings could be used to her advantage, if need be.

The experience of being a pirate's captive and having to submit to him by force, had begun to harden Annie. She had been a tender, young girl, only weeks ago. Now, she had become a woman baptized by fire. She had become ready for anything.

Annie scrubbed the dirt off her ravaged body with a cloth that hung on the side of the tub. She undid her braids, leaning backwards, knees bent and dunked her head in the water. Her hair felt coarse and oily. Her fingers worked to loosen up the knots and wash away the weeks of sweat and salt air. A bar of soap sat in a small tray, and Annie took it in her hands and began to rub it across her shoulders.

Uluj was getting that look in his eyes.

Annie tried to pay no attention, hoping he would lose interest. Once she felt sufficiently clean, she climbed out of the bath, trying to cover as best she could with her arms, but his eyes followed her exposed, dripping body. He handed her a cloth to wipe herself and patted the bed beside him.

She reluctantly sat and he took another cloth and wrapped it around her hair. She felt his rough hand caress her back and braced herself.

But then he stood up, stripped and walked into the tub, immersing himself in the water.

"Still warm," he sighed, eyes closed as he dipped his head back into the water, shaking his dark, curly hair.

The room was lit with candles and the soft glow made the muscles on his broad shoulders come into relief. Uluj, she acknowledged, was a handsome man. Despite herself, Annie admired his physique. His features, relaxed by the warm water, were fine and rugged at the same time. The wildness of the pirate captain was receding, and the chiseled lines of his face emerged behind the wild beard, tamed by the water.

Naked in the bath with his eyes closed, he seemed so much less menacing than the man who had captured her in violence and proceeded to brutalize her, night after night at sea. He almost looked vulnerable.

As she reached for her clothes, he opened his eyes, their blue irises twinkling in the candlelight.

"We'll have them laundered," he said.

Annie panicked. Her hand wrapped around her dress and without letting her gaze leave Uluj's, she imperceptibly searched for the precious vial. Once she felt it, she stopped and exhaled. She hadn't even realized that she'd held her breath.

"What will we wear?" she asked.

Uluj laughed.

"They'll have it ready by morning. Until then..." he gave her a naughty smile that made her stomach clench. As much as she began to see him more as human, he was still the pirate who destroyed her innocence. God only knew what he eventually intended for her. She couldn't lose sight of that. He was a man who had done her harm, but his potential plans for her could be even worse.

After taking his pleasure, Uluj turned to his side of the bed and quickly began snoring. Ever since Uluj told her that she wouldn't be able to have her clothes until the next morning, Annie had worried about Marina and their plan. But she had no way of warning Marina or communicating with her at all. She had to do something, had to meet her. But how would she walk out of the room?

Annie quietly climbed out of the bed and walked over by the bath to wrap herself in the bath towel. Her clothes had already been taken away to be laundered, so she had to think fast.

The noise from the tavern had quieted, and there was very little light coming from under the door from the corridor. Covered as best as she could she walked towards the door. The floorboards creaked and Uluj stirred in the bed.

Annie stopped. Uluj turned on his side and settled back in his sleep. She turned the doorknob and quickly sneaked outside. Soon after, she heard a door creak and a figure emerged. Marina!

"Shush," she said to her, and motioned her to go nearer.

Marina softly walked closer to her mistress.

"It can't be tonight; we must wait for our clothes to be returned. Go back to your room. Tomorrow is another day."

Marina nodded and the women sneaked back into their rooms to spend another night with their captors.

28 : Athanasios/Ioannis

1572

The young woman who'd stood in Georgia's kitchen had stirred something inside Ioannis that he'd not felt in a long time. It was a warmth, an anticipation, both primal and strong. As much as he tried to get her out of his mind, she was the only thing he could think of as he tended the animals, tilled the land, and gathered the crops. Especially late at night when he lay restless on the straw bed, in the room on the other side of the kitchen from George and Michaelis, Penelope's alabaster skin haunted him.

Georgia couldn't have been happy that he'd walked out while the two women were at her home, yet she'd never confronted him.

Why had he left when he'd had an opportunity to spend a little time with the girl who'd caught his attention?

He felt a strong pang of guilt whenever he thought about Penelope. And yet, at the same time, he felt joy when she entered his mind. Penelope!

She had a name, a beautiful name that he even dared to whisper while he was out in the fields alone.

Sitting on a rock to rest one late morning, he found himself whistling a tune and interspersing the whistling with her name. Penelope.

What was the guilty pang all about? Had there been another woman in his life before the beating stole his memories? Even if there had been, she and everyone else left behind the gates of Famagusta had been slaughtered. Maybe he should have mourned the unknown family he'd left behind. Names and faces, he'd lost, but their auras haunted his heart.

That night, returning from the fields, he'd felt a resolve.

After eating a plate of black-eyed peas, dressed with lemon and olive oil, accompanied by a hunk of hard bread, he sat on the stool by the hearth with his father and mother.

"I've been thinking..." he broke the silence.

Georgia and Michaelis turned to look at each other.

"What, my son?" said Michaelis.

Ioannis cleared his throat. Georgia fetched him a glass of water from the clay urn on the table and stood next to him, waiting.

He drank the water and handed her the glass.

"What if I had a wife in Famagusta? How can I marry again without even knowing?" he finally uttered.

The two older people sighed.

"It's been a difficult road for all of us."

Ioannis nodded.

"We're not going to bring any of them back, you know," Georgia finally said. "I understand how you feel. When you came into our lives, I wondered the same thing. Was I betraying my son by taking you in and by giving you all the care and privileges that belonged to him?"

She wiped her eyes with her apron.

"I finally decided that life is for the living, and God had dropped your broken body onto my threshold for a reason."

Ioannis looked at her.

"You needed a family, and we needed a son." For the first time since he'd arrived, Ioannis reached out and took the older woman's hand in his. He brought it to his lips and kissed it. Tears dropped down onto Georgia's hand and she wiped the young man's cheeks with her fingers. Michaelis rose from his chair and wrapped his arms around Ioannis's shoulders.

"You are our son now, and you have every right to be married and make your own family. Follow your heart, Ioanni. No one would blame you for that."

The family stayed entwined for a few more minutes. It wasn't something any of them were used to, but the emotions of that moment were overwhelming.

"So, what it is you want to do, Ioanni?" Michaelis spoke first.

"Could we talk about Penelope, Andriana's daughter?" Ioannis asked.

Georgia broke into a broad smile and pulled her chair closer to him.

"What do you want to know? She's a beauty. You saw her. Her parents will give her a piece of property, I'm sure of that, an olive grove perhaps so you can grow your own oil for the family. She's a good girl, skilled in weaving, knows how to keep a good home. She'll make a good wife."

Ioannis listened to Georgia's praises of the woman who'd awakened his sleeping heart.

"Do you think she would want me? After all, everyone knows I'm not really your son," he said.

Georgia laughed.

"Where else would she find such a handsome, hard-working husband? Haven't you seen how she looked at you?" Georgia tugged his sleeve.

"Shall I send word to her family tomorrow?" she dared to ask.

Ioannis nodded.

"Yes, let's ask for her hand," he decided.

That night, the only person who slept deep was Michaelis. Georgia tossed and turned as her mind raced over all the preparations she would be making for a wedding and Ioannis felt Penelope's young, slender body within reach of his embrace and his ambivalence put to rest by his parents' encouraging words.

The next morning Georgia sent word to the matchmaker.

Georgia prepared a mint infusion and set the glasses out on the wooden table.

"I'm glad you could come Marigo," she said offering her the tea.

Marigo sipped the infusion.

"I've been watching your boy, Ioannis. He's a hard worker, respectful and strong, and he's stirred up some interest in the village."

"I'm glad to hear that Marigo," she said unable to conceal a small smile. "But today, I called you here because we have a specific proposal we want to convey."

Marigo placed her glass on the table.

"Oh, really?" She said. "Who's it for?"

"We want to send a proposal for Penelope, Andriana's daughter." She let it sink in.

Marigo seemed at a loss for words.

"I.. she.. She's the most eligible bride in the village, Georgia," she finally said.

Georgia sat up and straightened her back.

"Maybe so, but we also have a handsome groom, hardworking and with his own property. They're a good match Marigo," she declared.

Marigo rocked a bit in her seat, picked up the tea and took a few small sips. She then placed the glass carefully back on the table and faced her hostess.

"If that's your proposal then I will convey it to her parents tomorrow. I will come back with their reply."

It wasn't long before Georgia, Michaelis and Ioannis had an answer: yes. Penelope's parents would be pleased to marry their daughter to Ioannis. It probably hadn't hurt that both mother and daughter had seen the handsome man at the house while buying eggs. The dowry was quickly settled by the skilled matchmaker. Penelope would be getting the olive grove next to her parents' house, a goat for milking, six clay dishes and two olive oil urns. Her father would build them a marriage bed. Her mother had been crocheting a large bed spread for her daughter's conjugal bed that would be ready for the June wedding.

They'd all agreed the newlyweds would be staying with Georgia and Michaelis, and eventually inheriting the small home.

The invitation for the betrothal came the very same day. Ioannis and his parents would visit Penelope's family that Sunday for a "getting to know each other" lunch and exchange of engagement rings.

Ioannis and his parents rose early to take turns washing in the small tub in their kitchen with water warmed at the hearth. They dressed in their clean Sunday clothes, the groom neatly attired, his beard tamed with a few drops of olive oil.

They arrived at Penelope's house, where her parents, the matchmaker and the local Greek Orthodox priest awaited to greet them. Once inside, they were seated in the sitting room. Penelope soon appeared, dressed in a red hewed long skirt and scarf, holding a tray of teas and sweet meats. She shyly offered her guests the refreshments, starting from Michaelis then to Georgia. When she reached Ioannis, she paused slightly and raised her eyes to him. Her imperceptible smile made it clear that this marriage was not only met with her parents' approval, but also her own.

Penelope put down the empty tray and took her seat next to Ioannis. The priest blessed the newly betrothed couple. After a lavish lunch, Ioannis and his parents took their leave.

Ioannis felt as if the Sunday of his wedding day would never arrive. On the first Saturday of June, his father sat him in the yard and trimmed his unruly hair and shaped his beard.

The next morning Ioannis walked towards the village church flanked by his parents. Clad in the black embroidered waistcoat that Georgia had made for her lost son, a long-sleeved silk shirt and the *vraka*, the gathered black breeches worn by men, Ioannis struck a handsome figure. A sprig of lemon blossoms pinned to his vest completed the wedding outfit.

The stone Church of Panagia of the Trapeza awaited them. Villagers stood outside, waiting for the couple to arrive for their wedding vows.

Ioannis beamed as Penelope arrived side-saddle on a donkey led by her parents and accompanied by other relatives and neighbors, singing wedding songs. The handwoven crimson wedding skirt and raw silk blouse that peeked through a black embroidered vest complimented her slender body. Underneath it all, he could see embroidered white pantaloons peeking between her long skirt and her pumps. The red bridal scarf, which set her apart from all the other women as the bride, held back her dark plaited hair. A *splinga* pin dripping with coral pieces adorned the scarf at the top of her forehead. Across her chest lay the multistrand *mirmidia* necklace, upon which small Ottoman coins, *skalettes* beads and a *trifourenio* filigree silver cross were hung. In her arms, she held a small bouquet of red poppies and yellow daisies with sprigs of jasmine.

Two men helped her dismount and, eyes downcast, she was led by her father into the stone church. Escorted by his parents, Ioannis followed, and they were both left side by side facing the altar. The lemon blossoms framing the Virgin Mary's icon at the entrance mixed with the honey aroma of the beeswax candles burning at the stands and became entangled with the age-old frankincense air of the Church. Ioannis' memory stirred for a moment, the scent trying to crack through the scars of his brain to the other side of this life. He squinted his eyes as if to see the light past the crack. The slanted rays of morning sun peeking through the narrow church windows gave his heart a tweak and then, as much as he tried, the memory proved elusive, and it folded into itself and disappeared back into the recesses of his damaged mind.

The villagers that had gathered outside for the wedding, filed into the church and took their places at the pews, men on the left side and women on the right. The priest, his tall hat and black vestments giving him an imposing look, stood at the front of the Holy Door adorned in his celebratory vestments, waiting for everyone to take their seats before starting the service. The cantors stood by their stands on either side of the Holy Door, ready to add their voices, whenever indicated, to the ritual.

Flanking each side of the couple were their bridesmaids and groomsmen, young people from the village, who stood in witness of the union.

Ioannis turned to sneak a look at his bride. He had only seen her three times before, once at the square, the other at his house, and the third during their betrothal. The earlier whiff of memory evaporated. He had never been this close to Penelope. It was as if his own body had caught fire; a fire he feared might consume her if he as much as touched her. She tilted her head slightly and looked at him through her long dark lashes. In her eyes he beheld the promise of love and understanding, the commitment of a long life together that she was bringing to the marriage. They held each other's gaze as the priest prepared for the service.

He felt the best man take his pinky and intertwine it with hers. As his skin tingled, he tightened his grip on her pinky, and she responded by giving a little tug.

Incantations from the altar soon began and he felt intoxicated by the chanting, the incense, the candles burning, and the closeness of his bride to be. The service proceeded and crowns of olive branches decorated with lemon blossoms were placed on his and his bride's heads. They were then crossed over their heads by the best-man and maid-of- honor until they were finally set to rest on their heads. Thin gold rings were exchanged and placed on their fourth finger of the right hand. The priest led them around the altar three times as was the ritual, each time pausing to kiss the icon placed in front of them.

Finally, as he and Penelope stood in front of the priest, they were given communion; sips of sweet wine mixed with breadcrumbs from a silver chalice and pronounced husband and wife.

Hand in hand, the newlyweds walked outside. Joined by their parents and bridal party, they accepted the villagers' congratulations at the Church entrance.

Ioannis held his new wife's hand and had a broad smile on his face as he accepted the good wishes. Yet, there had been a tugging inside him that he couldn't quite identify. The smile froze on his face. His grip on Penelope's hand slacked imperceptibly.

He forced himself to shake off the guilt, rid his heart of that moment of doubt, and, as Georgia and Michaelis had said, to go on with his life. The past was unknown. He had to look ahead.

29 : Annie

1571

After going back to bed, Annie had spent the first part of that night at the inn, restless. Her plan had not worked the way she had expected, and God knew when she and Marina would have another chance. By dawn, though, she succumbed to the clean, comfortable bed. With her stomach full and a bath for the first time in a while, she fell into a deep sleep.

A hand caressing her face startled her awake.

"Don't be afraid, my love," he said laughing, his handsome face relaxed.

Annie's heart was pounding, the nightmare of being captive returned her to the harsh true reality. She sat up in bed, tense and clutching the bed sheets to her naked body.

Uluj's face turned to a frown of concern. He took her by the shoulders and brought her close to him, encircling her in his arms. His masculine musk and the freshness of his recent bath was pleasing. How was it that this brute who had taken her and defiled her, had begun to stir a certain affection in her?

Fighting her thoughts of disgust, Annie eventually relaxed into his embrace, and he rocked her in his arms as if rocking a child, repeating, "Don't be afraid, my love, don't be afraid."

Her heart returned to its normal rhythm and Uluj held her at arms-length and leaned forward to kiss her lightly on the lips.

"Better now, aye?" he cooed.

Annie was torn between hating this man and succumbing to his charms. Was it possible that she could fall for him? And what about her wedding vows? What about her love for Athanasios? As young and inexperienced as she was, Annie began to realize that life could be very complicated. What she was feeling for Uluj was not love, but it was a sense that, if she had to be a pirate's captive, it may as well be with him.

"Come, let's go get something to eat," he said. "Look, our clothes are here!"

His demeanor on board his ship was always rough and serious and only during the nights had she sensed his capacity for tenderness. But now he was relaxed and playful.

As she got out of bed to pick up her clothes, he swatted her behind.

"And, if you are good, we could go and get you some new clothes!"

It was silly, she knew, but she almost felt happy that he would take her for new clothing. She had been wearing the same things for more than two weeks and she desperately wanted to wear something other than what she had worn during her abduction. She caught herself, however, getting too comfortable with being with Uluj and almost sharing in his enthusiasm.

If she wanted to be free of him and seek her husband, her father and her old place in life, she had to shake these unseemly feelings and refocus on her plan.

The two dressed and went downstairs where Marina and the first mate soon joined them. The two women exchanged looks, bringing their hands to their bosoms and discreetly stroking the tiny vial each had.

As soon as they walked outside, Annie suddenly stopped.

"It seems that I've forgotten my handkerchief," she proclaimed.

Uluj huffed but paused.

"Why don't you escort your lady to her room to fetch it," he finally said to Marina.

The two turned around and walked back inside and up the stairs to Annie and Uluj's room, where they shut the door behind them.

They took a moment to catch their breath.

"I never thought he would let us out of his sight," Annie finally said.

"Me neither," said Marina.

They moved to the bed and sat down, side by side. Marina's searching eyes were on Annie's.

"What are we going to do now?"

"We have to think this through a little bit more."

"Are we going to try to escape?" Marina responded.

"Of course, but we must have a place to go to. It isn't going to be safe for us to just leave."

"Why not? Why can't we just leave?"

"We are two women, alone. We have no money, no place to stay, and no protector. Well, besides the pirates."

Marina was quiet.

"Look at me," she said to the girl. "We will get ourselves free, but we must take our time."

Marina nodded.

"I'm so sorry, milady. I've let you down. I'm supposed to take care of you, but I don't seem to have done very well with that, have I?"

Annie took Marina's chin firmly in her hand and lifted it.

"We must figure out a way to escape and then find someplace to hide. But it must be fast. Uluj is not going to be staying here long."

Marina nodded again.

"Okay then. Let's go get ourselves some new clothes. Lord knows we could use them."

The group of four were back out in the dark tangle of the narrow alleys of the city, and after taking a few turns they arrived at a tailor shop.

As soon as they were let in, Uluj was greeted warmly, and a servant quickly ran for the proprietor.

"Master Uluj, how nice to see you again," the man proclaimed in French.

"It is good to be here, Monsieur Ansaldo," Uluj responded while they were all being shown to a sitting room.

"And who do we have the pleasure of meeting today?" Monsieur Ansaldo said giving an inquiring look to the women accompanying his client. Annie felt his eyes upon her and her clothing and immediately her face began to burn from a blush that rose deep inside her.

"This is Mademoiselle Annie de Lusignan and her lady's maid, Marina," he replied, ignoring the man's stares at the women.

"We are all requiring new frocks," he quickly told the man.

"But of course, monsieur," Ansaldo replied. "Let's bring the ladies into the atelier, where my wife will assist them with choosing their new clothes." He called his servant who escorted the women to the atelier.

The atelier was a large, high-ceilinged room, with tables of fine fabric of rich colors on long tables. A platform was set in front of a tall mirror next to which a slender woman, dressed in a long dress of taupe silk awaited.

She gave the women an intense look, and quickly proceeded towards Annie, with her hand extended.

"Mademoiselle, enchante," she said taking Annie's hand in her own two. "I'm Madam Dublas and I will measure you for your new dress."

Annie thought that perhaps Madam Dublas, had seen Uluj bring a few women for new clothes before. She banished the thought from her mind and allowed Madam Dublas to lead her towards the platform.

The rolls of luxuriously colored fabric that lay across the tables drew her eye, and Madam went over to them.

"Which one is your favorite?" she said lightly touching the fabrics.

"Do you like red velvet, or do you prefer the black taffeta?" she caressed the cloth.

Annie was mesmerized by the beauty of the fabrics.

Madam took a roll of the red, unfurled yards and yards and draped it over her client. Annie couldn't help but let out a small cry of joy.

Then Madam went back and brought out the black taffeta for comparison. She draped that fabric on Annie's other shoulder, and now, her reflection in the mirror really shone.

Madam stepped back and observed.

"The red is striking, my dear. It really brings out your milky skin."

She brought her hand to her head and tapped her forehead while keeping her eyes on Annie.

"Yet, the black taffeta is also so rich and luxurious. It sets off well your blond hair," she offered.

Annie was no nearer to a decision than before Madam's comments. She looked over at Marina, who seemed mesmerized by the newfound luxuries.

"I don't know milady. They are both beautiful!" Marina said.

"Oh, you are both no help," Annie said exasperated.

"Don't fret my dear, your escort said not to spare any expense for you. Why don't we make you a dress from each?" she said winking with a mischievous smile.

Annie couldn't help letting a satisfied smile play on her lips. Never before had she experienced such beautiful fabrics, and in an atelier in Genoa, she was simply delighted. At the Abbey, her father would send for silks from Venice for her, but nothing came close to this.

Madame Dublas took out her long measure and began to measure Annie's body dimensions.

"What is this nice pouch here, Mademoiselle?" Madam Dublas patted Annie's medicine bag.

Annie's hand flew instinctively to her bag.

"That's where I keep some herbs to calm my stomach," she said.

"And what about this little bump here?" Madam Dublas patted Annie's breast where the little vial rested.

Annie immediately yanked the woman's hand away and moved to step off the platform.

"Don't fret, my dear," she laughed. "I wouldn't have this clientele if my discretion wasn't assured," she added in a low tone. "We never know if a customer is running from someone or running towards someone."

She gave Annie her hand and helped her back up to the platform with a smile.

"High neck, sleeves gathered at the wrist, gathered skirts," she recounted and jotted down the specifics for the dresses.

Madame Dublas knew very well that she could use the most luxurious fabrics for Uluj and his entourage because the sumptuary laws of Genoa didn't much apply to him, as he spent little time there. She also didn't have to worry about the Tailor's Guild design approval since the clients would not be living in Genoa.

After Annie's measuring was finished, Marina took a turn on the platform. She chose a green taffeta with less color and shine than Annie's, but there was no doubt that the dress would be beautiful, and the finest she'd ever had.

The two women were offered tea, poured into the most delicate teacups, accompanied by small, hard sweets redolent of almonds and spices, unlike anything they'd tasted before. Madame Dublas informed them that the atelier had an army of seamstresses who would have the dresses finished by the next day. After all, this was a port city, and their clients were always in a hurry to embark.

Soon, they were reunited with Captain Uluj and his first mate who were getting fitted in the next room and the four exited the atelier back onto the narrow alleys of Genoa.

As they walked, Annie's arm supported by Uluj, her mind was no longer on the novelty of the luxurious new dresses, and the impossibly beautiful teacups. If she and Marina did not escape before Uluj decided to get back to sea, Annie realized that their fate would be back on board with the pirates. That would scuttle any hope of getting away from Uluj's clutches and reuniting with Athanasios and her father.

30 : Netta and Thanos

PRESENT TIME

Netta couldn't wait to drive to Bellapais with Thanos. Once they'd agreed during their coffee date on their plan, she had insisted they go the very next day. He would borrow his dad's car and come early in the morning to pick her up at her aunt's house.

That night, Netta had a hard time sleeping. Yes, she had been to Bellapais already with her aunt's family, and she had experienced there the visions that haunted her. Yet, the prospect of now going with Thanos, this young man who brought out so many feelings in her, was beyond her expectations. She was very excited about spending the day in Bellapais with him, yet there was another feeling lurking under this happy, youthful exuberance. She was torn between a happiness of getting to know him, and an unexplained sadness.

As she lay in bed, she tried to push down the sadness and savor the joy of what might be a budding love. She lay in her aunt's crisp sheets until finally she drifted to sleep. It was a tortured sleep, finding herself in a cabin on a ship at sea, feeling the vessel undulate as it plowed the waves, smelling the pungent odors of a boat, her skin clammy with the salty air. A young woman was with her and the two, dressed in long, full dresses and hand sewn shoes, were sad and afraid. By morning, all she remembered was the fear and the sadness.

Thanos arrived at her door at seven as they had agreed. She got in the car, waved goodbye to her aunt and cousin, and they took off for the checkpoint. The fear and sadness evaporated with the sunshine of the morning. Thanos' smile did the rest.

The journey followed the same trajectory as when she went to Bellapais with her aunt and uncle a week earlier.

This time, though, the feeling was as if she was returning to the place where she and Thanos belonged. Her anticipation to get there with this man she hardly knew and just met a few weeks ago was unexplainable to her, but it felt so right that she had to follow it where it would lead her.

Once in Nicosia, they drove to the checkpoint and handed their passports to the sentry who brought them inside his post to check them over. They were given their passports back and waved through. She heard Thanos release his breath as he stepped on the gas and sped away.

"That was hard for you," she simply remarked.

"You have no idea what it's like to have to hand over your passport to the Turkish occupiers of your ancestral lands. Humiliating! That's what it is."

Netta had never seen him so angry.

"I'm sorry you had to go through that," she said.

Thanos banged his hands on the steering wheel.

"Don't apologize for something that's not your fault. It's this damn situation with the Turks controlling our land for practically half a century. I feel so helpless because there's nothing we can do against an army of millions, a NATO equipped navy and air force. And what does the government of Cyprus have? National Guardsmen with puny armaments that can't defend against anything!"

"I'm still sad you feel this way," she murmured.

"I'm not mad at you, please don't take it that way," he said and reached his right hand over to touch her arm.

"I know, I know," she replied,

"Hey, we're going to Bellapais!" Thanos finally exclaimed. "Let's forget about those bastards and enjoy it!"

"That's the spirit!" Netta replied.

They had crossed the large expanse of the Mesaoria valley between the two mountain ranges and as they rounded the mountain pass, they got their first glimpse of the Kyrenia Sea. At the crossroads, they turned right. Above loomed the mountains of the Kyrenia range, the castles of Saint Hilarion to the west and Boufavento to the south, the Byzantine vestiges towering over the coast. She had read online that they had been originally built by the Byzantines as watch towers, looking out at sea as early warnings for Arab pirate incursions. From afar, they looked like they sprouted from the mountain itself, their towers and walls rising from the rock below them. The castle of Saint Hilarion came with stories of the Regina Eleonora, Queen of Cyprus, wife of King Peter I and mother of King Peter II. In revenge for his role in her husband's assassination, it was legend that she persuaded her brother-in-law to throw his Bulgarian bodyguards one by one out the large Queen's window of the castle and into the abyss below to their deaths.

The road began to rise up the mountain, towards Bellapais.

"Look at the houses lining the road, their blue shutters open to the street. You wonder who they belonged to before the Turks took over. It's kind of remarkable, really. This is the only place I've been to that is like that," Netta said.

Thanos nodded.

The two young people had developed an easy rapport and Thanos' anger had evaporated. Their mood now became more somber and contemplative, both seeming to be turning more inward as they neared their eventual destination.

"Can I tell you something weird?" he said.

"Sure," she nodded.

"The closer we get to the Abbey, the more I get this anticipation. I've been here before with my parents. Even though our family comes from Acheritou, Bellapais has always been a draw for us. But I've never had this feeling before. Weird right?"

She turned her head to look at him as he was driving down the winding road. His dark hair framed his face, his strong chin was firmly defined, his clear eyes focused on the road.

"Yeah, weird," she said dreamily. But not really. To her it was the same as she was feeling, this anticipation of getting there, as if by reaching the Abbey it would reveal a long-held mystery.

"Hey, did you know that the locals called the Abbey, *The Palace*? Yeah, because it was built by the Lusignans, the first kings of Cyprus who ruled from the twelfth century to the middle of the fourteenth."

"The Lusignans?" she asked.

"Yeah, the Abbey was started by French monks called the Premonstratensians, from Premontre France. They were White Canons, that's why the church is dedicated to the White Robed Virgin Mary. Aimery de Lusignan founded it around 1198. They were crusaders."

Netta rolled down the window and took a deep breath of the burnt wheat smells of the landscape.

"Cool. Yes, I've read about the crusaders owning the island and the Knights Templar. Richard the Lionheart owned it at one point, right?" she said.

"Have you read the history of Cyprus?" he asked.

"I've read a lot of the booklets the Cyprus Consulate sent me before I traveled," she paused. "Honestly, it's been hard to keep it all straight. There have been so many invaders, the island has passed from hand to hand, and I don't have it in my head yet. Do you know what I mean?"

Thanos laughed.

"Yeah, I do. It's hard to follow the whole story without doing an intensive study. So much has gone on here. There's so much history. A lot of turmoil, a lot of bloodshed, a lot of pain."

She was quiet for a while before she spoke again.

"Would it sound weird if I said that I feel the pain? There's a certain sadness I felt inside me when I arrived on the island. It became intense at Bellapais."

She looked at Thanos. His olive skin shone in the morning light of the Mediterranean.

His hands were strong but not too large. There was a fineness to them, as if he could just as easily play the piano as pick up a shovel. Netta felt safe with him, even though they'd only met a few times. The confidence he exuded inspired a sense of calm, reassurance, and well-being. She liked him.

"Not weird at all. So much happened here through the centuries, and really, in recent times with the Turkish invasion. Did you know that the Cypriots had an infirmary in the refectory during the invasion? Young women from the village nursed the National Guardsmen wounded by the Turkish army. You're probably sensitive to the historical pain."

"That's an interesting concept!" she exclaimed. "Do you think there is such a thing as being able to feel pain from another time?"

"Oh God!" he laughed. "I don't know for sure, but places do exude certain auras, don't you think? Like when you walk into a church you get this feeling, you know what I mean?"

Netta rolled her eyes.

"I'm not much of a church goer, so I'm not sure about that," she said. "I do agree about places having auras. Do you think it's the place, or the people who visit a place that can perceive things that may have happened there?"

"Well, it probably must be a combination of the two. A place with history and a person who has an old soul."

"Ha!" she said while waving her hand out the window to catch the breeze. "Are you saying I have an old soul, Mr. Thanos?" she teased.

His hands on the wheel, facing forward, Thanos replied.

"Yes, I do."

31 : Annie

1571

Upon returning to the inn, Annie noticed that people were rushing behind the bar, faces pinched and anxious.

"What is happening, Uluj," she inquired.

"The innkeeper's wife is having a difficult birth," someone next to them volunteered.

Annie immediately clutched her medicine bag. Grandmother had taught her about an herb used to ease labor in birthing women and it was part of her medicine trove.

"I think I may be able to help her," she turned to Uluj.

"Now what business does a lady like you have taking care of a birthing woman in an inn?" he replied.

"She needs my help Uluj, just like your crew did," she said coldly.

Uluj averted his gaze and shrugged his shoulders.

"Go," he offered.

Annie lifted the hem of her dress and hurried toward the bar. A door led to the backrooms of the innkeeper and his family. The smell of stale wine that permeated the tavern was strongest there, fortified by years of goblet fillings.

"What are you doing here, milady?" the innkeeper asked as soon as he saw her.

"I hear your wife is having a difficult labor," she said.

"She's been in labor since yesterday, and the midwife hasn't been able to help her. I'm afraid that if this goes on any longer, she and the baby may not ..." He lowered his head, wringing his hands.

"I may be able to help her."

"What could you possibly do for her? You are too young to know anything about childbirth."

"Bring me a cup with hot water." Annie said with authority.

The innkeeper paused for only a moment before ushering Annie to the room where his wife moaned and screamed. He rushed off to boil some water and Annie walked inside tentatively.

"What is she doing here?" the midwife yelled at the innkeeper.

"Maybe she can help." He looked at Annie and the midwife imploringly. The woman reluctantly nodded her assent.

"What are you doing here?" the midwife barked at Annie. "Can't you see this is not a place for a woman like you?"

"My grandmother was a medicine woman. I have some herbs that might help."

"We are past the time for herbs, my dear. I'm the midwife and even I am struggling to help."

The midwife's face was drawn, her eyes puffy and surrounded by dark circles. Bloody rags were piled on the side of the bed, and the birthing woman was writhing in the moist bedsheets.

"I can't guarantee you anything, but my grandmother always prescribed these for difficult births. I'll make an infusion with fenugreek and red raspberry leaf to ease and hasten her labor."

The hot water was fetched, and Annie unfastened her bag and took out the fenugreek seeds as well as the red raspberry leaves. Under the watchful eye of the midwife, she steeped them in the hot water.

"Here," she handed some of the fenugreek seeds to the laboring woman to chew on.

When the tea was well steeped, she tried to have the woman drink. She supported her damp head with one hand and brought the cup to her parched lips.

"This might help with your pain," she said as she coaxed her to take small sips.

Once the liquid was finished, Annie took a seat on a broken chair near the bedside. As time passed, the laboring woman's cries became less stressed, and her body seemed stronger. Annie could see from the midwife's lowered shoulders and smoothed brow that the birth was progressing in a better way.

It wasn't long after, when, with a primal scream and a final push, a baby boy emerged from the beleaguered mother's body.

Annie slumped back in her chair and let out a breath she hadn't even realized she had been holding. Her grandmother had taught her about the birthing herbs, but this had been the first time that she herself had ever used them on a woman.

The baby's strong cries brought tears of joy to the mother's face and her husband was soon joining them in the room.

"You saved them," he cried as he held his swaddled newborn son in his arms.

"Thank you," the exhausted new mother mouthed.

The midwife's eyes shone with gratitude.

Annie couldn't hold back the smile of joy on her face. She was proud to have been successful with her grandmother's legacy. Seeing the newborn life emerge right before her was a miracle and she was happy to have been part of it.

"I should go now," she got up to leave.

The innkeeper's wife struggled to sit up with the baby in her arms.

"If you should ever need anything, always know you can count on us." She lay back on her pillows.

"Anything," she repeated.

"Thank you," Annie said and walked out towards the tavern where Uluj and the others were sitting at a table.

Reluctant smiles greeted her as she joined them.

"So, how did it go, the birth?" Uluj finally said.

"A baby boy," she whispered as if she didn't want to disturb the newborn.

"Well, that's good news then! We should celebrate," Uluj remarked.

"Wine!" he ordered to the barmaid, and goblets of red wine were served to the table.

"On the house," the barmaid said, nodding towards Annie.

Uluj gave Annie a pleased smile and raised his drink towards her.

"To the Medicine Woman," he toasted.

The others followed his gesture.

"To the Medicine Woman!" They cheered Annie and drank.

Annie took a sip of the wine. Its warmth radiated through her body, and she felt it reviving her after her daring intervention. As she relaxed in her chair, it felt as if her grandmother's arms were wrapped around her, letting her know that she'd always had been with her.

The group of four stayed at the table, soon sharing a meal of fish soup. Annie had never tasted anything so delicious. The food at the Abbey always contained fresh vegetables, and on occasion, meat, but fish had been a rare treat for the hills of Bellapais. The garlicky broth seemed to be also flavored with fresh anise, and the chunks of white fish that floated inside mingled with onions that melted in her mouth. As much as she missed home, the novel flavors and sights she had been experiencing felt enriching. She guiltily enjoyed these newfound experiences, justifying that even if she didn't enjoy them, she would still be a captive. Denying these small pleasures would not change things.

What would change things would be if she and Marina were successful in escaping before Uluj ushered them back on board the ship.

Annie saw little opportunity for escape. Once the new clothing was picked up at the tailor's the next day, Annie didn't see how she and Marina would sneak away without being caught. And even if they did sneak away, how would they sustain themselves for the long trip to Venice? She shook her head and held out her goblet for more wine. As she indulged in the wine, she felt it loosen her mind and body. The people around her sounded otherworldly and distant as if they were filtered through a gauzy screen, and for the moment the cares that had hounded her every waking moment for the past week, seemed very far away. She'd just helped save a woman and her newborn baby, and that was all that mattered.

32 : Athanasios/Ioannis

1574

The infant squirmed in Penelope's arms, as two-year-old Georgia, grandma's namesake, played with a rag doll on the floor.

"He's beautiful," Ioannis said as he gazed at his young family. His parents and in-laws had been overjoyed when his second child was a son. His own happiness in this major event was a bittersweet reminder of the opaqueness of his past. Ioannis wasn't sure what legacy he was really providing for the innocent to the vagaries of the past, baby boy.

Even though he adored his family and the birth of his son brought him closer to his wife, his adoptive parents, his in-laws and fellow villagers, a shadow always hung over his existence.

He shook off the morose thoughts and smiled at his breastfeeding wife. Little Georgia toddled over to her father's chair and grabbed his leg. He picked her up in his arms. Her blond curls stood out from the other children's in the village, and so did her blue eyes, betraying Ioannis's dubious heritage.

He raised the child high in the air and let his worries get chased away by her giggles. It was late evening. The olive grove Ioannis received as a dowry was yielding a good crop, and the cotton they cultivated was beginning to sell at a nice profit. Yes, they were paying more taxes to the Ottomans, but at least he was providing for his growing family.

"You probably need to start thinking about adding that room to the house," said Michaelis.

"Yes, it's time to get to work before the third one comes along," said Georgia looking up from her crochet, a spun cotton blanket for the new grandson.

"Aye," Ioannis said still playing with his daughter. He looked at Penelope, her dark braids down her shoulders, her breast, white and full at the baby's mouth. He had come a long way from the day he was left for dead. Only faint scars on the side of his head and on his back remained to hark back. All that was left was the gnawing feeling that there was something he'd left undone, something waiting for him; something from his previous life.

His daughter shrieked and playfully pulled on his beard. The thoughts of another life disappeared. He rejoiced in the warmth of the family surrounding him and clutched his little girl in his arms kissing her blond curls and caressing her rosy cheeks.

"Let's gather some stones tomorrow, Father. Tomorrow is as good a time as any to begin building our new room," he said smiling.

The next day, Ioannis went with his father into their fields gathering stones to build an additional room for the growing family. It had been three years since he'd arrived in this village and already, he had put down roots.

"Father, what if we build two new rooms, one for the children and one for a store. We have people coming to buy our hens, eggs, olive oil and oranges. Perhaps it's time to make a room where we can keep everything we have for sale."

Michaelis let go of the stone he was pulling on and straightened his back to face Ioannis.

"Son, that's such a good idea!" He grabbed Ioannis by the shoulder. "Our products have grown and we're running out of room for them in the house. Your mother is always complaining about that."

The two resumed their work with increased vigor.

¤¤¤¤¤

Time had passed and the humble homestead of Michaelis and Georgia had doubled from three rooms to six. The room that had become the store was now a bustling place for villagers to shop. Through the years, the family had added bread that they got from the bakery, animal feed from a village grower, and tobacco. Georgia now spent her days at the store, with one or two grandchildren at her feet. Penelope, now in charge of the house, tended to the cooking, cleaning and washing that once was the purview of Georgia. The older of the six children were now able to help with chores, little Georgia in the house and young Michaelis in the fields.

At night, when Ioannis retired to his room, he'd lay his tired body on the bed next to Penelope, marveling at the life he had built. He had become a pilar of the small village society, evidenced by the prominent seat he was afforded in church on Sundays, as well as by the invitation of the village elders to join them when they had important decisions to discuss.

Having supportive parents and being married to a loving, hardworking woman had been important for Ioannis' success. In addition, the Ottomans gave the Cypriots the right to own property, cultivate it, and pass it down to their heirs. They'd also encouraged them to cultivate the land and trade the surpluses, as Istanbul had been growing in population and needed to import more food. These important changes were what made Ioannis and his family thrive.

Over the years, the feeling lurking in the recesses of his mind of something lost, something from an unknowable past, had receded, and only occasionally did it creep up in the night to impinge on his happiness.

33 : Netta and Thanos

PRESENT TIME

The car pulled into the square of Bellapais, where the Abbey's belfry came into view. Netta, had now made the same journey to Bellapais that she had made with her aunt's family. It was the same, yet she strongly felt that this journey was significantly different. What was it about Thanos that made Netta feel as if she had known him before, as if she belonged right there, next to him?

The familiarity belied the short time they had known each other. Was this what they talk about when people say love at first sight? Netta didn't know. What she knew was that there was something very special about this man and their connection to each other.

She and Thanos got out of the car and walked towards the ancient edifice. They crossed into the small area behind the belfry and soon walked in front of the cloistered garden with the tall cypress trees and the arches.

They looked at each other and continued to the covered walkway that surrounded the three sides of the Cloister.

As they walked the length of the loggia, Netta felt an electric aura envelop them. Suddenly, she was running on the green of the cloistered garden, giggling and calling out to the boy who was chasing her. Her dream was alive again and she played with abandon. The boy's hand grabbed her shoulder, and Netta turned to look at him. For the first time in her life there was a face there.

It was Thanos.

34 : Annie

1571

Annie, Uluj and the other two members of their party went up to their rooms to rest after lunch and the morning's shopping and the excitement with the Tavern owner's birthing wife.

After a short rest, Uluj got up and got dressed. Annie watched him from the bed.

"I'm going out for a while," he said when he noticed her gaze.

Annie nodded.

"I won't be long," he added. Annie shrugged her shoulders.

"Where are you going?" she finally asked.

"I have some business to take care of," he answered.

"Like what?" Annie persisted.

"Nothing for you to worry about," he smiled and came over to give her a caress on her cheek. "Make yourself pretty, we'll go for a stroll later," he said as he left the room.

As soon as he exited, Annie jumped from the bed. She ran to the dresser and got her clothes. She dressed quickly and made sure the vial she so closely guarded was still in its place. She listened carefully as Uluj's footsteps grew further and further away. She gave him a few more minutes and slowly cracked the door, carefully peeking out her head. Uluj was nowhere in sight.

Annie, tiptoeing down the corridor and the steps to the Tavern below, walked determinately towards the back of the place, same way she had done earlier in the day, when the birthing woman needed her help.

She opened the door behind the bar and walked towards the Tavern owner's rooms. Once inside the kitchen, Annie stopped.

The new mother was lying in a day bed set near the hearth, the young one swaddled in a clean cloth in her arms. The new father was also there, standing over his wife and son.

"I'm sorry to disturb you," she offered as they noticed her entering the room.

The innkeeper brought her a chair.

"We're happy to see you, milady," he said, his wife smiling and nodding in agreement.

Annie took a seat.

"Something we can do for you milady?" he asked, giving her a careful look.

Annie opened her mouth as if to speak and closed it again.

"Is everything alright?" he persisted.

Annie shifted in her chair and leaned towards the man and his wife.

"I need your help."

¤¤¤¤¤

Uluj returned from his outing and found Annie dressed and ready to go for a walk. He summoned his first mate and Marina and the four of them left the inn for a stroll outside, as he had promised her.

After they exited the inn, they turned away from the port, towards the Cathedral of San Lorenzo that dominated the hillside. Annie couldn't get enough of the sights of this city. To her it seemed like a magical place with a great number of people living there and an endless number of homes, built one next to the other with high walls rising from the street, with no front yards. She liked the wide piazzas that surprised her as they appeared after long narrow streets with almost no sunshine breaking through. She adored the colonnades they walked through as they strolled across the piazzas. The four walked in silence, taking in the sights around them.

They climbed higher up the hill, the streets meandering. If she were to be left there she wouldn't know how to get back to the inn. She looked down towards the sea and could see that the city was built like an open shell facing the Mediterranean Sea.

"You haven't seen anything like this before?" Uluj asked.

"No," she replied. "Bellapais is a small place compared to Genoa. Only a few people live there. The village is only a few houses."

"How do you like Genoa so far?"

Annie smiled.

"It's so big, I've never seen so many people together before. It feels like it's going on forever. And it's so rich! Look at all the goods being loaded and unloaded at the port!" she marveled.

"Where are we going?" Marina dared to ask.

Uluj stopped walking.

"See that bell tower up there?" He pointed with his hand. "That's the Cathedral of San Lorenzo, a great big church built of marble and decorated with beautiful statues and frescoes."

Annie looked in the direction where his hand was pointing, and she could see the bell tower that had been visible from the ship before they had disembarked. She took a deep breath, took a long look at Uluj.

"I can't wait to see it," she exclaimed and began walking again towards the church.

They arrived at a large piazza, at the opposite end of which stood the magnificent edifice, its tower rising high into the blue sky. The sun was traveling lower on the horizon, and Annie could see its rays striking the large rosette above the front doors of the building.

"Here it is!" Uluj announced triumphantly. "The Cathedral of San Lorenzo consecrated in the year of your Lord 1118."

Annie couldn't get enough of the multifaceted façade. The three entrances, with the grand center entrance towering under the rosette window, were fashioned in black, white, green and red marble. The large arches of the side doors were scalloped hemispheres of alternating black and white. She could find no comparison between the massive wooden doors and the main entrance to the church of Panagia the White Robed, of Bellapais. The extraordinary scale, the opulent materials, the intricate carvings of the marble were unmatched.

Uluj led the way inside. Annie had not been in a church since that fateful night when John had come to her chamber to whisk her away at the charge of Athanasios. A day had not gone by that she didn't think of her husband, of what had become of him and what he would think of her after all that had happened between her and Uluj. She had been innocent when she left the Abbey. That innocence was now behind her. No longer the naïve, sheltered daughter of Henri de Lusignan, the inexperienced betrothed of Athanasios, she had grown so much in the past three weeks. There she was, in the fabled city of Genoa, walking up the narrow alleys, entering the most magnificent structure she had ever experienced in her life.

Annie looked down at the long expanse of the church from the entryway and felt dizzy at its length. The black and white marble floor shone in the dwindling sunlight creeping from the windows at the nave at the end. She looked at the colonnade that stretched across either side of the endless corridor. The marble columns glistened. They were topped by black and white marble apses, all the way to the nave. She glimpsed beautiful niches on the sides of the church past the colonnade, with statues of Christ framed by towering winged angels. She looked up to see the intricate carvings that decorated the walls, walls so high, she felt they soared into the sky. The splendor of this church, she could never have imagined in her former, sheltered life.

She could see that Marina was equally bewitched by the magnificence of the cathedral. They were silent as they perused the niches, the carvings and the statues. Annie sidestepped from the center aisle into a row of pews. She dropped to her knees and bowed her head in prayer. Marina joined her and bowed next to her. The two men accompanying them proceeded ahead towards the nave.

"I'm praying very hard, milady," Marina whispered without moving.

"We're going to need a lot of blessings, Marina," Annie whispered back.

"I'm ready for tonight, no matter what happens. I'm not afraid," Marina said.

"We've got to be as ready as we can," Annie replied.

Uluj and his mate were now turning back, so the two women fell silent.

The men patiently waited for Annie and Marina to finish their prayers before they escorted them back outside.

"What did you think of that church, ladies?" Uluj asked. "I may be Muslim, but it's true that my mother was Christian."

"Magnificent," Annie replied, with as much enthusiasm as she could muster. Uluj offered his arm, a pleased smile on his face and he and his first mate escorted the two women back to the inn.

As night fell over the port of Genoa, the teeming streets became increasingly quiet. The only sounds came from a weary worker's shuffling steps home, the musings of a few drunken sailors, and the tolling of the church bells signaling the last Mass of the day.

It was past nine, and Annie, Marina, Uluj and his first mate were finishing their evening meal back at the inn.

35 : Athanasios/Ioannis

1591

Twenty years had passed since Georgia and Michaelis had dragged the broken body of the beaten man inside their little home, dressed his wounds and saved his life. The truth was that he had also saved theirs. With their own son dead and no other family of their own, they thought that they would be destined to live their old age alone and with no one to care for them. This man they'd found had changed their whole lives. His marriage to Penelope wove him into the fabric of their small community, his children filled their house with sounds of joy, the small house expanded with the family, and the fields and orchards were now well tended and prosperous. At the time they rescued him, they hadn't imagined how things would turn out.

The children, now older and with the firstborn girl, Georgia, of marriageable age, her beauty and her dowry making her a sought-after bride, Ioannis was proudly thinking about his family as he raked around the olive trees, cutting back the weeds.

"Come to the house, quick!" said Penelope, panting, her braids askew.

"What's happened?" Ioannis asked, alarmed at the look in her eyes.

"Just come," she grabbed his hand and led him up the path and back to the house.

As they crossed the threshold, he saw his father sitting in the corner, with his head in his hands. The children were unusually silent.

"What's happened?" he demanded.

Penelope guided him to his parents' bedroom.

Georgia lay in her bed, her thinning white hair plastered to her head, her mouth crooked, and her eyes unfocused and narrow.

"Mother!" he cried as he reached for her hand.

"She can't hear you, Ioannis," his wife said. "She's been like this since her siesta. Your father called me in. She doesn't talk, she doesn't listen."

Ioannis let his hand drop.

He hovered over the bed, looking at the woman he'd called mother for two decades, the grandmother of his children.

"Mother," he whispered, softly taking her hand in his.

"Did you send for the healer?" He turned to his wife.

"Yes," she said, "Our Georgia went to fetch her, but I don't know what she could do."

Penelope's hands kept pulling on her apron, constantly smoothing it and tugging at it. She finally sat at the edge of Georgia's bed and ran her hand gently over the ailing woman's forehead.

A loud moan escaped Georgia's mouth, her eyes searching Penelope's face.

"I'm here Mother," she said in a soothing voice. "I'm here. I'll bring something that will feel good." And she rose to fetch a wet rag to cool Georgia's face.

Ioannis buried his face in his hands. Georgia had been a very loving mother to him, and it was hard to watch her suffer.

His wife returned and motioned him to go see to his distraught father.

"Father," he said as he walked towards Michaelis. "Father," Ioannis laid his hand on Michaelis' bony shoulder. He and Mother both had aged since that fateful night in August, but he'd never noticed it before. His father's sunken shoulders barely held his head aloft, and his gnarled hands couldn't hold steady.

"What's wrong with her, son?" asked the old man, his eyes sunken and bloodshot.

"I don't know, Penelope sent for the healer."

"She's been like that since afternoon," he sighed.

Ioannis sat next to him, keeping his hand on his shoulder.

"You think she'll heal her?" he raised his head.

"Don't know, Father, don't know."

The healer arrived; an old woman with her creased face half hidden in her scarf and a bag of herbs draped across her body. After she touched Georgia's face, picked up her slack arms, and spoke to her without response, she asked for warm water to make an infusion. They tried to get Georgia to drink some of the herbal infusions, but she couldn't swallow. The healer and Penelope made compresses and rubbed the old woman down. As the night passed and the family huddled in the small kitchen around the hearth, waiting, Georgia fought for her life.

"I think it's time to fetch the priest," the healer said.

Penelope squeezed her husband's hand.

"Send Michaelis," she said.

The young man took off in the night and soon returned with the priest. He brought the chalice with the holy communion and donned his ceremonial stole to give Georgia the last rites.

She passed away in the dawn hours, her family around her.

The neighbor women, clad in black, their braids undone, arrived and began to lament and sing the mourning songs, a sacred part of honoring the dead. After Georgia had been washed, anointed and dressed by Penelope and the healer, she was wrapped in her funereal shroud. By morning, she was placed in a pine casket in the home's main room. Villagers streamed in and out of the room, paying their respects to the dead and to her family. The close relatives stayed to keep vigil with the family.

By mid-day, the grave had been dug. A procession, led by the priest and his cantors, carried the casket to the cemetery. Georgia was laid to rest in the same ground where her own parents had been buried. After the small funeral, the family returned to the home, now bereft of its matriarch.

They sat around reminiscing, and grieving.

"What's this? Penelope emerged from the old woman's bedroom.

In her hand was a small round object, in the shape of a ring.

"Let me see that!" Michaelis took it in his hand and turned it around.

"I think it's stone," Penelope said.

"We found this on you that night," Michaelis said holding the ring and pointing it towards Ioannis.

"What? You found this on me?" He grabbed the stone ring. As soon as Ioannis touched the cold smooth surface of the ring, he felt a jolt, as if there was a straight line from the ring to his heart.

"Why didn't you tell me about it?" he asked.

"We didn't think it was anything, just a piece of stone." Michaelis motioned towards it.

"But this was on me, when you found me?"

"Yes, we found it in your clothes. We thought it was nothing."

"You should have told me," he solemnly said.

Michaelis reached out to his son.

"Forgive us, Ioannis, we didn't know any better. Georgia thought it was nothing."

"I could've..." Ioannis started to say.

"We thought it was nothing," the old man pleaded.

Ioannis noticed Penelope watching. He pocketed the ring, as she opened her mouth.

Michaelis motioned her not to say anything. Ioannis, shoulders hunched, walked outside. His wife gave him a moment and then went out to him.

"That stone ring was important to you," she said standing close to him.

He nodded his head.

"What would have happened if they had given it to you back then," she asked.

"I don't know, Penelope," he sighed. She reached for his hand.

"Sometimes I feel like there's a curtain in front of me hiding my previous life. As much as I try to lift it, I'm never able to see behind it. But the sad thing is I do know that it's there."

She squeezed his hand.

"This ring might have been a clue as to who I was back then, before..."

"Yes," she said. "But today, I know exactly who you are."

He turned to face her.

"You are my husband, the father of my children and the son of those old people who loved you dearly."

"I know," he said, "It's been a lifetime and I've never regretted our life together, it's just that sometimes it gnaws at me, and I would've liked to know. That's all."

Penelope gently took the ring from his hand.

"Let's put this away in a safe place for our children. We'll show it to them and tell them that it's part of their heritage."

"Yes, it's part of their heritage. Maybe one day, we'll find out exactly what that is." He said and put it into a wooden box in their armoire.

36 : Annie

1571

Night gently draped its cloak over the narrow alleys of Genoa. The din of men barking orders at port workers, of barrels squeaking on the stone wharf, of seagulls squalling as they dive for scraps, of footsteps rushing down the street, had quieted down. Bits of conversation caught in the breeze faded away into the folds of darkness.

Uluj had been especially tender with Annie that night. Annie had even allowed herself to gently caress his broad shoulders and strong chest.

"Shall I pour you some tea?" she asked as she got out of bed and walked towards the small table in the room.

"Tea, at this hour?" he said.

"It's a soothing blend that the innkeeper's wife gave me as a gift for helping her with the birth," she responded, a barely perceptible stiffness to her words. Her back to Uluj, she kept her hand suspended over the small glasses.

"In that case, I'll have some." He rolled over on his back and rested his arms over his head.

Annie poured the tea in both glasses. She wasted no time. She deftly retrieved her vial, hidden earlier in the afternoon inside the vase on the table, and tipped it over into one of the cups.

"Where's my tea?" Uluj said playfully.

"Coming right away, kind sir," Annie responded in a similar tone, while trying to steady her shaking hand. "Here you are," she offered him the drugged goblet, looking at him directly in the eyes. No cloud of suspicion, no sense of apprehension resided in his look.

Annie sat at the edge of the bed next to him and took her goblet in both hands.

Uluj sat up in the bed, his torso propped by the pillows and cradled the goblet in his hands. He brought the steaming brew to his nostrils and took a whiff of the aroma.

"Well, let's drink up then," Annie said before she brought her tea to her lips, her eyes still focused on him.

Uluj raised the tea to his lips.

"When did she give it to you? I don't remember you saying anything about it," he said.

Annie held her tea close to her lap, wrapping her fingers around its round contours to keep her hands steady.

"She sent it up to the room while you were out, silly," she responded giving him a playful side look.

"Of course," he said, raising the glass and taking a sip. "Mmm, it's good," he murmured, drinking some more under her watchful eye.

As they sipped and chatted about picking up their new clothes the next day, embarking on the ship soon after, Uluj's eyelids began to droop, and his speech slowed to practically a slur. She thought she saw a questioning in his look before he fell back on the pillows. She gently removed the goblet from his hand and placed it on the table.

Annie dressed as fast as she could.

"Mmm."

She jumped and turned towards him, discovering Uluj moaning in his stupor and flailing his arms. She paused to lean over him as he lay on the bed, looking vulnerable. Quickly straightening her body away from him, she turned back to her preparations; she finished dressing and wrapped her few belongings in a shawl. She reached inside the vase and extracted the vial that had been her constant thought through the times of her captivity. She placed it back in her bosom, draped her medicine bag across her body, hefted her bundle and swiftly opened the door to the hallway.

Her trusted maid, Marina, stood there quietly, clutching her own bundle of belongings.

"It worked, milady!" Marina whispered excitedly. "It worked!"

They furtively descended the staircase to the tavern hall and scurried across the floor towards the door behind the bar, where the innkeeper beckoned. They disappeared through the door and entered the back rooms where the innkeeper and his family lived. Marina was seeing these rooms for the first time, and she looked around the squalid quarters in dismay. It made Annie notice anew the smell of stale ale reeking through the dank rooms and the dirty rags and broken furniture that were strewn about.

"Hurry," the innkeeper called and ferried them through a small creaky back door out to an alley. A fetid smell hit her nose, and Annie raised her shawl to shield herself from it.

"We are in your hands now," Annie said as they followed the innkeeper down the maze of alleys. The two women followed dutifully, knowing full well that their lives rested on the aid of this grateful man they knew nothing about.

As grateful as the innkeeper and his wife were for helping with the birth of their child, there was no knowing what kind of people they were and what they might be willing to do for a few extra lire. Two women of obvious higher standing might be considered a prize bounty. As an innkeeper, he would have had many opportunities to be an intermediary in unsavory business for his clientele. They had taken a great risk and were at his mercy.

As Annie contemplated this risk, she also was keenly aware that if they had not escaped that night, their chances of ever escaping the pirates would evaporate. Once they were on board the ship once again, escaping would have been impossible. The risk of being sold into slavery once Uluj had tired of her was real, as was the risk of the two of them becoming separated at some point. This opportunity was the best option they had.

They could barely see ahead of them, as the innkeeper had not brought a light for fear of being discovered. As a native, he knew those dark winding alleys well. Annie and Marina made sure to keep close.

Surrounded by the sounds of scurrying vermin that surely dwelled in the bowels of those massive buildings, it seemed they had walked for hours in the darkness.

When they stopped for a moment, Annie gripped Marina's hand and Marina squeezed back in silence. They were still not safe, they could be discovered at any time, so it was important to push on.

The innkeeper continued walking, back and forth in the labyrinthine streets, for what seemed like miles. Their eyes had grown used to the darkness and they could make out little creatures darting through the alleyways in a frenzy. Both women held their screams, for this was a matter of life or death.

They crossed open piazzas and walked under colonnades. The innkeeper turned a corner and stopped in front of a worn wooden door in the back of a church. He rapped his knuckles against the wood twice. He stopped, waited with his hand still raised and then knocked again twice.

A shuffle could be heard inside. The sound of a latch drawn, and the door cracked open. A woman's face, draped in a white and black wimple peeked through.

"They're here," was all the innkeeper said and the nun quickly opened the door wider, looked down the street both ways and ushered them inside.

"I'll be going now," the innkeeper said.

"Bless you, Senor," the nun replied and closed the door. The silence in the place was so total, Annie felt as if the world had stood still. She gripped Marina's hand and the two of them followed the silent nun through the dark corridors towards what they hoped would be their salvation. Bellapais had been a monastery, but the bustle of monks and their families around the place meant there was always noise emanating from within its walls.

The nun stopped in front of a closed door. A faint light underneath the threshold drew a straight line across the bottom.

She knocked lightly and waited, looking at her charges with a look that said, *be patient*.

"Enter," came the reply.

She opened the door and motioned for the two women to pass through.

Behind a large wooden desk sat a woman dressed in the same habit as the nun who'd let them in. She was visibly older and at first glance it was obvious there was something that set her apart, a certain aura, a certain nobility. Her chin was held up high, outlining the fine contours of her nose, and her torso was straight as if a board had been affixed to it. Her gray eyes were focused on them, and they shone with a bright, kind light. A large gold cross hung on her chest.

The nun who'd let them in, hurried towards the older woman, curtseyed and kissed her hand.

"Good evening, Reverend Mother," she said. "I've brought the young women."

The Abbess placed her hand over the nun's head and proceeded to give her a blessing.

"May the Lord be with you Sister Grace," she said, and the young nun rose and left the room, leaving Annie, Marina and the Reverend Mother alone.

The Abbess beckoned the girls to go near.

Annie and Marina stared at the desk where this imposing woman was seated.

"Come, come, don't be afraid," the Abbess finally addressed them.

Annie rushed over and dropped to her knees. Marina followed quickly. Annie felt the Abbess's hand rest on the crown of her head. The weight of the woman's hand imparted a benevolent sensation that radiated all the way down Annie's body, and she was surprised to feel the fear and anguish she had been feeling receding. She stayed there, head bowed, her shoulders relaxing with every passing second.

"Let me look at you, child," the Abbess said, and raised Annie's chin up with her index finger. She looked Annie in the eyes and Annie felt that those bright, gray eyes held the sort of kindness that she needed.

"You can stand up now, child," the Abbess said. Take a chair, both of you," she motioned. "Let's figure out what we're going to do with the two of you."

37 : Annie

1571

Annie poured out her story to the Abbess. Marina, sitting by, nodded her tear-streaked face at every turn of the events that had brought them to the Convent.

The Abbess was a patient woman, who carefully questioned her new charges about the man who'd abducted them, the circumstances under which they were abducted, and their background in Bellapais. Her lips tightly pursed, and her eyes closed as Annie confessed the especially brutal parts of her story.

Once Annie was done recounting, the Abbess rose from the chair behind her desk and approached. She placed her palm over the woman's head and gently caressed her hair.

"You are in our care now, Annie," she said. "There is a powerful force looking after both of you here. You're safe."

Annie broke into sobs. For the first time since their capture, she let herself grieve for the life she'd lost and for the damage that had been done to her. The nun stood over the young girl until all the crying was drained out of her and her body, exhausted, went limp. Marina cried as well, but Marina had often sobbed into Annie's arms, releasing some of the anguish that had been accumulating in her body as their captivity went on. Annie had been the one who had to be strong and never showed any weakness during their ordeal. Now, in the sanctity of that holy place in the safety of the Convent, she allowed herself to empty her pain.

Annie and Marina were given a spare meal of porridge and taken to the sleeping quarters.

The next morning, Annie was awakened by a distant hymn echoing in the chambers of the Abbey. She sat up in the narrow cot where she'd spent the night and took a moment to collect her memory.

She looked around the small bare room and relief washed over her. She had broken free! She had escaped Uluj and his band of pirates, and the certainty of enslavement that would have awaited her. She hugged her body. She was safe.

She rose from the bed and followed the sound of women's voices singing through the corridors of the convent. The singing led her to the entrance of a chapel. A candlelit aura surrounded the kneeling nuns, their black habits highlighted by the white of their wimples. Dawn had barely broken through the narrow slits of the chapel windows. It reminded her of waking up early to go down to the Vasiliki with her grandmother to secretly gather the medicinal herbs.

Annie walked to the threshold of the chapel and dropped to her knees, putting her hands together in prayer. She was thankful to God for her escape. She also prayed for the brave innkeeper and his family, who had delivered her and Marina to safety. She prayed suspicion would not fall on him. She prayed that her husband and her father were safe.

Soft footsteps behind her turned out to be Marina, who had also been awakened by the chanting. The two young women kneeled side by side, bowing their heads and letting the otherworldly song wash over them, as if cleansing them from the things that had been done to them in the hands of the pirates.

None of the nuns raised their heads from chanting to look at the newcomers. Only the Abbess, who sat in her special seat briefly raised her eyes and Annie thought she saw a glimmer of approval before she went back to her prayers.

The prayers ended and the nuns filed silently out of the chapel. As she passed the entrance where Annie and Marina stood, the Abbess signaled them with a nod to join the line of nuns.

The group reached the refectory without speaking. It was a cavernous space, furnished with long wooden tables and chairs. At the head of the room sat a table on a platform where the Abbess sat with two other nuns of high rank; the Prioress and Sub Prioress, Annie figured.

Several nuns stood at the heads of the tables, ladling a steaming soup from a black cauldron into the bowls set on the tables. Baskets of dark bread were placed in the center. When the smell of the fish soup hit her nostrils, Annie felt her stomach lurch and she realized how hungry she was. She glanced at Marina who was focused on the steaming bowl in front of her, waiting for someone to say grace before picking up her spoon.

When all the bowls were filled, the Abbess put her hands together and bowed her head in prayer for the food they were about to receive.

The nuns followed suit. The dining room reverberated with the sounds of metal utensils on ceramic bowls, garments shuffling and women eating, as soon as the Abbess completed the blessing and picked up her spoon. The nuns around her now lost some of their somber demeanor and spoke to one another in gentle, soft tones.

Annie was grateful for the nourishing food but also for the nurture. Among this group of women, she felt a safety she hadn't felt since her abduction. The soup warmed her body and her soul. She took special note of the nuns sharing her table, a lot of them young like her. A sister next to her passed the basket of bread and smiled as Annie took a piece and placed it by her bowl.

"Welcome" she said gently.

"Thank you," Annie replied, feeling a pleasure so genuine that she realized how much she had hidden of herself with Uluj.

Once the meal was finished the Abbess motioned for Annie to follow her out of the refectory. Marina made a step forward, but the Abbess raised her hand signaling for her to stay. The two walked the long corridors in silence, the Abbess' habit sweeping the stone floors behind her, her staccato footsteps echoing down the halls.

The Abbess stopped in front of a door she unlocked with one of the large keys hanging from her belt. She ushered Annie inside and Annie recognized the office she had been brought to the night before. The Abbess sat behind her desk and Annie took her seat facing her.

"How are you feeling today, Annie?" the older woman asked.

"Much better today, thank you," Annie responded, all the gratitude brimming inside her for the kindness she had been shown.

“So, now that you are safe, we have to decide what we are to do with you and your maid,” said the Abbess crossing her hands in front of her on the desk.

At Annie’s questioning look, she continued.

“Where do you want to go from here? Where are your people, who can we contact for you?”

Annie now understood that they were to plan the next step in their escape. Unless she and Marina left Genoa, or never set foot outside the Convent, there was always the risk that Uluj would find them.

In her mind ran the events of the past month, between the time that she’d been whisked out of the Abbey to the boat that took her to Athanasios, her furtive wedding on the seashore where she was united with her beloved by two stone rings tied together with a red ribbon that she still managed to keep, to the fateful voyage towards Venice and her capture by the pirates. All those happenings brought her here, in the cloistered rooms and corridors of this nunnery in the middle of Genoa, with her captor probably already released from the effects of the tincture of the deadly Nightshade Belladonna that she’d sprinkled in his drink. Annie had never before deployed that most powerful of medicines her grandmother had taught her how to make. Grandmother would always caution her about the use of that tincture.

“It’s probably the most important tincture you could make, but also the most dangerous. It must be used only in the most pressing circumstances. It can be deadly, but it can also be a lifesaver.”

Her grandmother’s words echoed in her mind as she took stock of the events that brought her here, to this moment.

It was time to decide her own fate, something she'd never been allowed to do before. Grandmother and Father always made decisions for her. And, it would have been her husband, Athanasios, who would have made the decisions had their lives not taken this unexpected turn. The circumstances, though, had changed all that the traditions dictated, and there she was, a woman, alone and vulnerable in a strange city, having to decide what her next step would be.

Hadn't she already begun to make her own decisions when she plotted her escape with the innkeeper? Annie realized that, once she'd taken that step and asked for the innkeeper's help, once she'd planned it and worked it out with Marina to tip those miniscule vials into the pirates' drink that night, for the first time in her life, she had taken her fate into her own hands.

"Annie my child," the Abbess' voice shook her out of her thoughts.

"Yes, Reverend Mother," she replied.

"What should we do with you and your maid, child?" she asked once again.

Annie was now ready to reply.

"I had been on my way to Venice, Reverend Mother." She said, "My husband had made arrangements for me there. However, those arrangements were made through his emissary and our escort, John, who was also on the ship that the pirates took. His fate is unknown to me."

With those words she searched the Abbess' face for any answers to her dilemma.

The Abbess took a few minutes before she spoke again.

"You cannot stay here. Even if you were ready to join our order, the danger of you being discovered could put us all in jeopardy."

"I understand, Mother." Annie replied.

"I've been thinking about you all night and praying for a solution to come to me," the Abbess said.

Annie waited expectantly.

"We have a sister order in Venice." The Abbess continued. "We can safely transfer you and Marina out of Genoa to Venice. If you agree, I will contact the Abbess there. In the meantime, because even in the confines of these walls, there may be prying eyes, you and your maid will don the nun's habit to blend in."

Annie was nodding her head in agreement. She and Marina would be secretly transported to Venice dressed as nuns.

"What will happen to us in Venice?" she asked.

"I will suggest that you stay at the convent until we find your people. The Order will make discreet inquiries about them." She smiled at Annie.

"Do you have any information at all about who we may be looking for?" she added.

Annie racked her mind to glean any information that Athanasios or John may have shared with her that, at the time, she did not pay too much attention to. She regretted her reliance on the men, and her trust that all would be taken care of by them. She wished she had asked more questions about her destination and the plans for her stay in Venice.

But wait, there was a sliver of information she recalled. Athanasios had said he was sending her to family. She didn't know where they lived but she did know the name of the family: Cornaros.

¤¤¤¤¤

Annie knew the story of Caterina Cornaros very well. Caterina Cornaros had been the last Monarch of Cyprus. After her husband's death, Caterina had been Regent to her son James III. Once James died as a child, Caterina ascended to the throne in her own right. Caterina had been a cousin of her grandmother. Stories of the last Queen of Cyprus were her grandmother's favorite tales while they sat by the fire on long dark nights in the Abbey of Bellapais.

She regaled her little granddaughter with tales of Caterina's Court in Nicosia, where she had spent some years before her daughter married Henri and came to live with him in Bellapais.

"I wore dresses of Venetian silks so intricate I have never seen the likes of them since I left the palace. They were specially made for us by seamstresses brought from Venice. I remember dressing for balls filled with dancing and music. We wore strings of pearls whose luster rivaled the stars."

"Ah," Annie's grandmother would sigh, reminiscing of those glory days before her Queen cousin was forced to relinquish her throne and return to Venice.

The Cornaros family was renowned in Venice and Annie was certain that Athanasios had contacted them on her behalf to secure safe accommodations for her in Venice. Caterina Cornaros was long dead by then, but her name and her family remained.

"Do you know the name of your people, my child?" the Abbess asked.

"Cornaros," Annie uttered. After a few seconds of standing silent, the Abbess raised her hands to her face and sighed as if coming out of a trance.

"Ah, child," she said. "I had a feeling that I had in front of me a young lady of renown. We'll find your people. Go to your room and rest now. I'll let you know when we have more information."

Two days had passed since that conversation and Annie and Marina, dressed in the habits of the nuns, blended in as best they could with the other nuns. The rough clothes were a bit of a relief for the women, as they'd been able to escape with only a few items of clothing. They felt safer and less of a target in those dark and ordinary habits.

Annie was asleep in her room when she was awakened by a soft tap on the door.

"Enter," she said, and the door squeaked open. The Abbess stood in the doorway accompanied by the nun who had let them into the convent three days earlier.

"Reverend Mother!" Annie jumped from bed and stood before the older woman.

"Get dressed and gather your things quickly. We have secured passage for you, tonight."

Annie's eyes opened wide. As she quickly dressed in her nun outfit, her mind was going two ways. On the one side Annie was relieved to be finally leaving Genoa. On the other, though, the safety of the convent had been an oasis in the desert of her circumstances in the past month and she was reluctant to let go of it so soon.

"Are you alright, my child?" the Abbess asked.

"Yes. Yes, I'm fine, Reverend Mother," she answered, her voice shaking.

The Abbess walked over to the girl.

"You're going to be safe, Annie. We'll make sure of that."

They quickly grabbed her bundle and met Marina in the corridor.

"Let's go my children. We've got to hurry."

Annie and Marina were ushered into the Abbess' office. Two seated men jumped up as they walked in. Their rough tunics were tied around the waist with a leather belt. A scapula, the long wide piece of woolen cloth worn over the shoulders with an opening for the head, was over the tunic with a cowl attached. Their heads were partly shaven on top.

The Abbess removed a letter from her desk, its red seal visible as she approached the men and handed it to one of them.

"Guard them as if they were your own."

"We will, Mother Superior," said both men and bowed respectfully.

She raised her hand over their heads and drew the sign of the cross.

"Bless you and your mission. May God be with you all," she said. Her aide opened the door and Annie found herself back in the dark alley she had escaped through only three nights before. This time, instead of the innkeeper, she and Marina were escorted by the two men.

They both reached up to make sure their wimples were secured over their heads, shielding their faces as much as possible from any prying eyes. Even though it was very late in the night and most people of Genoa were asleep in their beds, there still was the possibility of spies looking for the two runaway women.

The four of them turned towards the port, back the same way that they had escaped only a few days before. They hurriedly walked the cobblestone alleyways, the moonless darkness being their friend and their foe. Their dark vestments were also a blessing, keeping them hidden from anyone up that late at night.

In what seemed, to Annie, like forever, they arrived at the port and hurried towards a vessel. In the middle of night, it had its sails unfurled and seemed ready to fly as soon as the mooring lines were released from the port posts. The rope ladder was still down, and the men helped hoist Annie and Marina unto it before scaling it themselves.

Hands stretched out and helped them onboard.

"Welcome aboard, sisters," a man in a large hat and dark jacket over a white shirt said, bowing slightly and kissing her hand.

"I'm captain Georgio," he added.

"Pleased to meet you, sir," Annie replied.

"We're off to Venice tonight, leaving a bit earlier than planned," he smiled. "We'll get you there in one piece, don't you worry."

He motioned to one of the sailors to come over.

"Take the sisters to their quarters."

He tipped his hat as Annie and Marina were led away.

Once in their cabin, the two women removed the oppressive wimple and sat on their beds digesting the events of the night.

"Here we are again on a ship headed for Venice. The last voyage did not end well, so I'm scared, milady," Marina said to her mistress.

Annie looked around the small cabin and found a jug of water with two glasses. She poured some for each of them. Marina rushed to help.

"I can do that for you milady!" She tried to take the jug away from Annie.

"It's alright, Marina," she said. "I should be able to do a few things for myself."

She looked up at the girl, who looked disappointed.

"Not that I don't still need you, Marina. I always will," she reassured her.

They sat back down on their beds and sipped their water.

"I'm scared too, Marina. But whatever comes, we must face it."

"I wish we could have gone by land." Marina said.

"That is just more difficult and dangerous. The Abbess said that by sea is our best route."

¤¤¤¤¤

Annie was up on deck as they approached La Serenissima. Magnificent palaces rose off the water, their colonnades impossibly ornate. Churches larger and grander than anything she had ever seen before in her life were dispersed among the buildings. She had been awed by the beauty of Genoa, with its church spires and tall buildings. Venice though, was an even more spectacular sight! The storied city of her grandmother's memories lay before her like a splendid lady bedecked in her most exquisite silk and pearl dresses.

Marina joined her as the ship navigated the Lagoon, going deftly around the small islands and nearing the giant palace that Annie realized had to be the Palace of the Doges.

Both women drank in the marvelous sight of the city of water, the splendor briefly eclipsing their worries.

Once the ship docked at the edge of a grand piazza, the two women with their male escorts disembarked. They found themselves in a city with large piazzas and massive buildings. As they left the piazzas they were led through narrow alleys until they stopped at the gate of a large edifice. One of their escorts knocked.

The enormous door creaked open, and a sister appeared.

"Can I help you?" she asked.

"Take us to your Abbess," one of the men replied. "We have come from Genoa and have a message from the Abbess of Santa Maria de la Gracia." He produced the sealed message.

The sister quickly moved to the side and invited the party to enter. They followed her to a large chamber where she motioned for them to take seats at wooden benches.

"Wait here," she said and walked away.

She returned shortly and silently escorted them through the halls of the convent until they stopped in front of a large door. She knocked and they all entered the room.

A nun sat behind an ornate wooden desk, a large cross dangling from her neck. A painting of the Virgin Mary holding the infant Jesus hung on the wall behind her. She motioned for them to approach. One of the escorts moved closer to the desk, bowed slightly and produced the sealed letter from the Abbess.

"For you from Mother Francesca, Reverend Mother," he said.

"Thank you," she replied and with a wave dismissed the nun.

"Please take a seat," she invited her guests and slit the seal open with a small knife.

The Abbess then turned her attention to the message she just received.

Looking up after reading the contents, the Abbess smiled at the group.

"Welcome, sisters," she addressed Annie and Marina. "We are glad to have you here."

Then she turned her attention to the men.

"Thank you for bringing them here safely. You can stay at a cottage on the premises, until the next ship sails for Genoa."

With that, she opened the door and summoned the nun who'd been waiting outside to escort the men to their quarters.

The Abbess returned to the women.

"Annie, tell me about your relatives. Are they expecting you?"

"I'm not sure, Reverend Mother," she sighed.

"Why is that child?"

"I was told that arrangements had been made for me in Venice with my relatives, but as you probably know, our ship was overtaken by pirates, and our journey interrupted. I imagine that the family of Cornaros is expecting us."

The Abbess, sitting behind her desk placed her hands together and looked at her for a long moment.

"You will stay with us until we contact your family to collect you. You are safe here," she assured her.

The two women were escorted to their quarters where they could clean up and rest from their journey.

38 : Athanasios/Ioannis

1614

He missed Penelope. She had been dead almost five years, and the house felt empty without her puttering around. The fire she tended for cooking their meals had long been out and the bed they'd shared for almost fifty years was cold and desolate.

He missed Penelope.

Yet, in the deep folds of his heart, where the mystery hid of who he'd been, he missed another. It had always been there, this absence. It got smaller as he married, and even smaller after he had children, tended his fields, raised his animals. But the void had never completely gone.

After Penelope died, time opened in front of him as a large expanse and the dull ache of that mysterious longing returned. At first Athanasios mistook it for his grief and longing for his wife. As time ticked away, he began to discern it as the other, the different yearning; the one that came before, the one that made him wonder.

Time rose and fell, and often, as he sat alone at twilight at the threshold of his house waiting for the sun to set, he felt as if his mind was expanding beyond the space that Penelope, the raising of a family and, the struggle for a living once occupied.

At times he felt as if he could almost glimpse behind the curtain of his fractured memories, into that other self. A fleeting image of a blond girl passed through and just as quickly disappeared. She resided in the cavern of his broken mind, etched there permanently, but elusively. He'd reach out to touch that precious figure, but as much as he tried, she was always just an arm's length beyond his reach.

Ioannis was almost sixty-nine.

"That cough sounds bad, Father," his son would say every time he hacked.

"I'm just fine," he would reply.

Ioannis' legs dragged now, and he barely shuffled from room to room. Finally, one morning he could no longer get out of bed.

As he lay there, struggling to breathe, his energy spent from the long years of toiling the fields, the blond girl returned to him. She stood next to him on a beach, their fingers entwined, a red ribbon trailing.

His mind, free of chores, children, desires, expanded into the time stretching before him and found the pieces of himself that he'd left on that doorstep that cruel, pivotal night in 1571.

As his breath became shallower and more labored, he reached deep into the folds of his mind.

He saw their hands adorned by stone rings, tied with red ribbons, binding them together.

He struggled to speak.

"What is he trying to say?" His children around the bed looked at one other, as their father hadn't spoken in days. "He must be hallucinating."

"The ring," Ioannis managed.

"Wait," his first born said. "While I was rummaging through grandma's old things, I found a box. A box with a stone ring."

"The stone ring," Ioannis barely whispered.

His daughter raced to the next room and soon returned with a little box; inside of which lay the stone ring.

"Look, there's also a paper," she said.

"What does it say," the others demanded. She unfolded the old piece of paper.

"This stone ring was found on Ioannis in August of 1571, after the fall of Famagusta, when we found him on our doorstep, beaten unconscious and almost dead by the Ottoman soldiers. He never regained his memory."

His daughter took her father's gnarled hand tenderly into her own and placed the ring in his palm.

"Here Papa, here's your ring," she whispered in his ear, gently caressing his withered face.

Ioannis' features softened as he wrapped his fingers around the contours of the stone. He brought his hand to his lips and gave the ring a weak kiss.

"Annie!" he cried. "Bellapais! Annie!" His last breath floated above the bed, over the mountains towards Bellapais, as his hand fell to his side, his fingers releasing the stone ring that rolled across the bed covers.

39 : Annie

1571

Annie and Marina had arrived on the shores of Venice only the day before. The first glimpses of it overwhelmed young Annie and her maid.

The Abbess summoned Annie to her office in the late afternoon. She and Marina had retired to a room where they'd washed and rested. A tray of soup and bread had been delivered to them for lunch.

"I have excellent news, my child," the Abbess greeted her as she entered the room.

Annie waited.

"Your relatives are delighted to hear of your arrival. They are sending a gondola with an escort to take you and your maid to one of their palazzos. I explained that your, ahem, misadventures on route brought you to us."

Annie's shoulders relaxed and she let out a deep breath. The Cornaros family had been expecting her, after all, and now she would be taken in by them.

"Thank you for your hospitality and for making the inquiries with my family for me," she said to the Abbess with a small curtsey.

"Not at all, my dear," the Abbess replied. "I'll send for you as soon as they arrive."

Annie returned to her room until she heard a knock on her door.

"Miss Annie, your gondola is here," she was summoned.

She and Marina were escorted to the Abbey's boathouse. The black gondola, its graceful narrow shape reflected in the calm water, its prow and stern turned up, was tethered to the land. The women were helped in and seated in its plush seat. The gondolier stood behind them navigating the busy waters of the city with a long pole. They were ferried across the canals, gliding under elegant bridges and passing by grand palazzos rising out of the water. They watched people walking in the streets of Venice before finally arriving at the boathouse of a grand residence.

"The master would like to see you," said the liveried servant who helped them disembark.

Marina was taken to the servants' quarters.

Annie followed the servant to a large drawing room, resplendent in its silk covered walls and its crystal chandeliers. She instinctively brought her hand to her head, covered by the nun's habit. What would her relatives think?

A large man stood by the fireplace; his back turned. His blue velvet cloak shimmered in the candlelight. The fine embroidery of his protruding sleeves contrasted with the blue of his cloak.

A woman in a sea-foam green brocade gown, her sleeves long and fitted with white, ruffled cuffs, sat in an armchair to his right. The fitted bodice was decorated with a gold band and black lapels and a strand of pearls, adorned with a square pendant of gold, rubies, and pearls. Her square décolleté was edged with a standing white ruffle and she wore a double strand pearl necklace with a ruby pendant. Her upturned hair was held away from the face with a gold band. A large, sheer, white veil was draped over her head that created a curved shell shape around her torso.

The man turned towards Annie. She stopped and gave a small curtsey, as her grandmother taught her about palace etiquette.

"I am Georgio Cornaro," he said simply, "and this is my wife, Elizabeth." Elizabeth gave her a small nod as she fanned herself with an orange and yellow feather fan. Georgio motioned for Annie to take the blue velvet-covered seat to his left.

"Welcome to Ca Cornaro," he continued. "You can stay here for as long as you need. You are family and we'll always take care of our family members."

Annie took a seat.

"Thank you for your kindness to me. I don't know what I would have done, where I would have gone..." she said.

Elizabeth rang a small bell and a servant appeared with a large silver tray that he placed on a table nearby. It was set with delicate glasses filled with red wine and offered one to each person. Annie took a sip of the rich, fragrant liquid. It was a salve in this strange new land she had found refuge, among these people who took her in, relations, yet still strangers to her.

The Cornaros family graciously settled her and Marina in the rooms of one of their homes. The opulence of those rooms and the palace itself was striking and completely new to the young women.

Large paintings adorned the silk covered walls, and gilded furniture was arranged around the rooms. The pastel silk fabrics that covered the settees and armchairs seemed to sparkle in the candlelight at night and their softness was comforting and luxurious. The large windows, opening onto the city afforded them views of the large piazza below and of the people who walked past, in all their splendor.

Annie and Marina had never seen so many servants bustling around, especially ones dressed in fine uniforms. Their nuns' habits were taken away and they were replaced by fine silk dresses. Even Marina was furnished with two fine frocks. Not as fine as her mistresses but certainly finer than anything she had worn before.

"Today you rest. Madam will visit you tomorrow," Annie was told.

A hot bath was prepared for Annie, and Marina helped her bathe. It had been a welcome relief after the travails of ship sailing where water was scarce and only a small bowl was available to wash their faces in the morning. The warm water and the olive oil soap that washed her body was as if it melted the traumas she had lived through in that previous month. A lavender oil was also provided for her, and Marina rubbed it over her lady's limbs, scenting the young woman's body. Marina combed Annie's long blond hair like she used to in the days at the Abbey when they were both still innocent.

40 : Annie

1571

"I wonder what's happened to my father," Annie said to Marina as the days passed without word from Bellapais. "And no word of Athanasios, either."

"They'll be joining you, milady, don't you fret," Marina soothed her.

The Cornaros name opened doors for Annie in Venice. As a relation to Caterina Cornaros, she was welcomed into Venetian society as if she had always been one of them. As the sympathetic young woman from Cyprus, with her looks and manner- fresh and exciting to Venetian society- she had many invitations.

A month of anguished waiting passed until news arrived that her father had managed to escape from Bellapais and would soon join her.

Annie couldn't wait for him to arrive on Venetian soil. When his ship came to port, Annie was there waiting with Marina.

"Papa!" She fell into his arms as soon as he disembarked.

Henri embraced his only child and tried to suppress his sobs. His cheeks were sunken, and his hair had turned fully gray. His clothing was dirty and rumbled. Annie's papa was not the powerful leader of the Abbey she'd left almost two months earlier.

"You're alive!" he said, clutching her.

"And so are you, Father!" She cried, tightening her grip on the frail man.

Father and daughter held on to each other for a long while.

"We must go," the attendant who'd escorted Annie finally said.

"But please tell me. What of Athanasios?" she pleaded as they disentangled their embrace.

"Not now, child," he averted his eyes.

Annie's stomach clenched.

They were whisked to the palazzo where Annie resided.

Her father was taken to his rooms to change and rest.

Annie was left standing in the drawing room, her arms limp by her sides, her mind not wanting to believe what her heart already told her was to come.

She waited anxiously and when Henri finally emerged, she was sitting in the salon.

Annie motioned him over. He approached and took her hands in his.

"I bring terrible news. Famagusta, the last bastion of Cyprus, has fallen to the Ottomans."

Her eyes wide, she waited.

He reached into his pocket and produced an object that he placed in her hand. She felt as if her heart had been cleaved in two when she recognized the pendant she'd hung around Athanasios' neck.

"Noooo," she moaned as she brought the pendant to her lips. "No!"

Henri placed his hands on her shoulders as if he could steady the storm that was boiling inside her.

"I'm so sorry," he said.

Annie began to rock back and forth, and her sobbing filled the room.

"How? When?"

"His body was found, badly injured but they recognized his clothes, and the pendant was around his neck. There was no doubt it was him."

"A stone ring? Was he wearing a stone ring?" she desperately asked him.

"What stone ring, child? I heard nothing of a stone ring," was his answer.

"But he promised" the young girl cried. "He promised he'd come for me!"

"I'm sorry child," her father tried to comfort her.

"Maybe it wasn't him? How can you be sure?" she sobbed and collapsed on the floor. Marina gently gathered her up and took her to her room.

¤¤¤¤¤

As great as Annie's grief was, the missing ring had left a glimmer of hope; an unreasonable, unfathomable sliver of chance that Athanasios might still be alive.

In her short life, Annie had already suffered more than anyone she knew. Athanasios' loss had been the blow that topped even her suffering at the hands of the pirates. Only Marina and she knew of that defilement and humiliation.

Annie had shared with her father her story of leaving Bellapais, arranged by Athanasios. She had told him of her marriage on the shore and her subsequent boarding of the ship to Venice. But the part of her story that took place between the time she boarded that ship to the time she arrived in Venice, remained hers alone. How would her father take the news that his daughter had been violated by the most hated pirate of them all? And how would he treat his daughter after such disclosure? As much as she loved her father, she really wished her grandmother was still alive to give her unconditional love and advice.

Numerous invitations kept coming for Annie, but she accepted only enough so as not to create a stir. Henri was understanding of her grieving for Athanasios, her beloved since childhood. Yet, as a father, he was anxious for her to remarry and settle in comfort and stability.

A few weeks after her arrival in Venice, Annie had thought something was not quite right. Her grandmother had talked to her about monthly womanly bleeding that began when she was twelve, and explained that once she was married, her menses would stop when she became pregnant. With the worries and fear of escaping Uluj, and her grief over Athanasios' loss, Annie didn't have much time to think about those things. But now, she calculated and recalculated only to come to the same conclusion. Her menses had stopped.

"I'm pregnant," she told Marina, the only person in whom she could confide.

"Oh, milady!" was all Marina could muster.

Annie shook her head.

"Athanasios was my first. It could be his, Marina. I feel in my heart it is his."

"What will you do, milady?"

"I have to tell father that I am with child."

As soon as Henri heard his daughter's revelation, he immediately contacted their benefactor, Georgio Cornaro.

"My daughter was married to a brave warrior just before she escaped Cyprus," he confided. "He perished in the battle of Famagusta, and she is with child. What shall we do?"

Georgio took a few moments before he spoke.

"She is a beautiful woman and there are already a lot of patrician men who've been inquiring about her."

"Indeed," Henri concurred. "What shall we do?"

"I have a plan."

41 : Annie

1571–1623

Annie's silk embroidered gown shimmered in the pale sun of the Venetian spring. Her long hair, wrapped in golden ribbons, lay loose about her shoulders. She rested her delicate hand on her father's arm as he escorted her in the procession along Venice's Piazza San Marco, that would conclude in her becoming the wife of Niccolò Benedetti.

The wedding dress, made of rich golden brocade, showcased her young bosom, and the tight cinching hid the faint thickening of her waist.

When her father had summoned her to his rooms and announced his arrangement to give her in marriage to the scion of a Venetian patrician clan, decades older than her, she protested.

"Please Father!" Annie pleaded. "Don't do this!" She fell to her knees and gripped the hem of his robes.

Henri was unmoved. Yes, he had been young and in love once. His heart had been filled with emotions for his beloved. But he could not have a daughter whose marriage, on the sands of a war-torn beach, could only be attested to by a servant.

"You must understand. You cannot have this child without a husband at your side. All of Venice will shun you."

"But what if Athanasios is still alive? We have not found his ring, Father. Please, let's wait a while."

Henri lifted her tear-soaked face to him.

"The time has passed for that. There can be no more waiting, Annie." He sighed.

Annie sobbed.

"Athanasios is gone, my child. He's gone and you must accept that."

"No!" she rose from the floor. "I feel it in my entire being. He's alive, Father!"

"Come now, Annie. Calm down. You do realize it yourself. There's no time left for waiting. Once your condition shows, all your prospects will be gone, and we will never be able to show our faces in society."

"No! I don't care!"

"And what of your child? What kind of life do you want for that child?"

Annie stopped crying and stood quietly facing her father.

"Do you want people doubting his legitimacy for the rest of his life? You must come to your senses. Think of that child!"

Annie collapsed on the nearest chair. She realized that she had no choice but to acquiesce to the arranged marriage, brokered by Georgio Cornaro, her benefactor.

After her wedding, she and her maid moved to her husband's family's palazzo. After the first night together in his bed, the aging aristocrat did not show must interest in his new bride. And that was just the way Annie preferred it. She was young, and she understood that her youth and vigor would be buried in this marriage, but the sacrifice was worth it to save her child, who she hoped was Athanasios's child, from Venice's scorn.

She and Marina waited anxiously until the months passed and the baby was born. After he was placed in the arms of his mother, and her mother-in-law and the midwife left, she and Marina gently unwrapped the swaddling and gazed at the naked newborn. Annie caressed his strong limbs, gripped his well-formed hands and ran her palm over the wispy blond fuzz covering the top of his head. The baby boy twitched under her touch. Annie wept. Without doubt this was the son of Athanasios. They easily passed the child to her unsuspecting husband and his family as his own. She named him Athan.

¤¤¤¤¤

In the year 1623, a woman lost in the bedcovers of a big canopy bed, her frail frame laboring the last hours of her life's journey, faintly moved her lips.

"What is it, Mother?" Her son, Athan, said. Her lips moved, yet the sound was too faint for him to hear.

"Tell me, Mother," he said inching even closer to her and placing his right ear by her face. He saw her mouth move again and as he strained, she said.

"Stone ring, Athan take it. Go to Bellapais."

Athan immediately drew back for a moment. He neared his mother's face again as if wanting confirmation of what he'd just heard.

Her hand on the silk bedspread opened and closed as if seeking something desperately.

"Stone ring, Athan."

He rushed to her dressing table and rummaged for the stone ring he'd seen there many times. Even though he'd sometimes catch his mother sitting there and putting the ring on her finger and stroking it tenderly, whispering to it things too low for him to hear, he'd never really thought much of it.

"Here it is, Mother," he placed it in her clawing hand, the joints swollen with years. He folded her stiff fingers over it, and he thought he'd discerned a smile on her thin lips as the cold stone seeped into her palm. In her eyes the prism of time reflected the truth of a decades-ago true love that bound her to her beloved by the red ribbon of fate.

"Bellapais, Athanasios. Stone ring. *You* must bring to Bellapais!"

Athan froze at these instructions from his dying mother. He drew back from her bed. A brilliant light hovered over Annie, and for a split second, it was as if the arches of a Gothic building reflected in that light. In the sky above them, Saturn and Jupiter, in their orbital embrace, set the course for the Great Conjunction.

The planets in the sky above them had only aligned for that moment. The light he saw around his mother grew more brilliant, folded into itself and disappeared. Athan was left wondering if he had hallucinated the entire thing.

With that, Annie's mouth went slack, her bony fingers relaxed, and the ring rolled out onto the silk folds of the bedding.

42 : Netta and Thanos

PRESENT TIME

As Netta and Thanos drove away from the Abbey, the great arches getting farther and farther in the distance, the tall cypresses becoming smaller, Netta felt as if she were leaving a magical land that had loomed large in her dreams ever since she could remember.

Pulling out past the outpost, over the demarcation line that seemed to separate the past from the present, she felt a sadness coupled with an inevitability. What had she really expected was going to happen if she went there? The dreams and visions had been strongest while there and her connection to Thanos became amplified while on the grounds of the Abbey. It was as if he and she were tied to some mysterious story that had taken place there eons ago as two children playing tag in the Cloister.

She fumbled in her pocket for her stone amulet. She ran her finger around it, feeling its smooth cool edges. The fear and anxiety that had gripped her as they sped away from the Gothic relic seemed to ease as she caressed the stone ring. Ever since her mother had given it to her as a child, it had become her go-to soother and it didn't fail her again that day.

Thanos, as if sensing what was happening to her, reached over and placed his palm over her hand.

"It's always the hardest leaving," he said echoing her own feelings.

"You feel it too?"

"Ever since I first went there with my parents and grandparents, I've felt this incredible sadness when I must leave. As if I'm leaving a part of myself there."

"That's exactly how *I* feel!" Netta said, the fingertips of her free hand still on the ring.

No one was home at her aunt's house.

"Just as well,"Thanos said. "Let's go for a coffee."

"I would like that," Netta agreed.

Thanos guided her towards the nearest café.

Seeking privacy, the two chose a table where they were away from other patrons.

"What happened to you back there?" he said to her.

Netta's hand still worried the stone sitting deep in her pocket.

"What do you have there?"Thanos asked, motioning his head towards her hand.

"Oh, nothing." She said and pulled out the ring. "Just a stone I like to play with. It makes me feel good." She laughed.

"Let me see that," he reached for the ring.

Netta pulled back playfully.

"Why? It's like my security blanket." She giggled. "I know I'm a grown woman, but I still need it." She looked at him coyly, palming the ring.

Thanos' eyes gazed back at her with a serious look.

"Can I see it?" he pressed.

She opened her palm slowly.

"I think I may have seen that ring before," he said.

"Really? Where?"

"I don't know."

"How is that possible?" she said.

Thanos kept staring at her.

Netta opened her palm and offered the stone ring to him.

Thanos turned it over in his hand completely absorbed.

"My great aunt has one that looks just like it." he said. "How is this possible? How do you have this ring?" He said as if he was talking to himself.

Netta raised her shoulders.

"I got it from my mother. She had gotten it as a child from her mother. It was the only thing she had from her family, and she wanted me to have it. I just always cherished it."

"My great aunt has one just like it," Thanos repeated, as he still turned the ring over.

Immersed in their own private story, they hadn't noticed the wild haired woman who'd stopped by their table.

"Asimose," she demanded, her palm proffered.

"The gypsy!" Netta exclaimed, her hand flying to her mouth.

Thanos made an annoyed motion for her to leave.

"Asimose," she persisted. "I will read your palm."

Netta quickly pulled out a coin from her bag and placed it in the woman's palm.

"I remember you," she told her. "You spoke of a building with big arches."

The gypsy woman ignored her and grabbed Thanos's hand and turned up his palm.

For a long moment, she traced his lifeline with her dirty finger.

"You lived," she said without looking up. "You lived a long life. Athanasios, your mind may have forgotten Annie, but your heart never did." She stared at them both with her fiery dark eyes outlined in kohl.

"Your mind may have forgotten her but your heart never!" With that she dropped his hand and walked away into the street crowd.

Netta and Thanos sat stunned for a while.

"You know her?" Thanos finally asked.

"No! Not really. A couple of days ago while I was waiting for Toula, she appeared out of nowhere, like today, and told me my fortune. She spoke of a church with big arches and a man from whom I'm separated by time and a long sea."

She looked at him.

"I don't have any idea what she meant; she disappeared just like she just did. She said he'd come for me."

Thanos put his cup down and looked at her as if wanting to say something and then changed his mind.

"What? What is it?" she asked.

"Is there someone you're waiting for?" he said awkwardly.

Annie laughed.

"No, there's no one."

She turned the ring around in her hands.

"This is going to sound crazy."

"What?"

"I've always felt as if there was someone out there. You know, I've had these strange dreams of the Abbey, even though I'd never been there before. I had this one dream, so many times."

She paused.

"Go on," he prompted her.

"I'm a little girl running in the Cloister with the tall cypress trees and a little boy is chasing me. Whenever I turned around to look at him, my dream would stop. I never got to see his face."

Thanos was silent. Netta looked at him quizzically.

"What?" she said.

"It doesn't sound crazy to me at all," he finally said.

"Except for today," Netta said. "Today at the Abbey I had the vision, but when I turned, I saw him."

He reached across the table and took her hand.

"Who was he?"

"It was you," Netta said softly.

"Oh, Netta! *This* may sound crazy, but I've had a similar dream. Not many times in my life, mostly when I was a child. But since I met you, the dream has come back."

Netta squeezed his hand, nodding.

"I'm a little boy chasing a little girl in the Cloister. She's got blond curls and she's laughing and we're both shrieking. Just when she goes to turn her head back to look at me, my dream stops."

Netta pulled her hand away.

"You're just making that up." She said, her face suddenly ashen. She rubbed her shoulders as if she were cold and sat staring at him.

"I swear, Netta," he reached for her hand again. "I'm not making it up! I used to tell my mother about it when I was small, but she always said it was just a dream."

"This is just too much coincidence for two people who've never known each other until this summer. Somehow, it's really, really, weird," she said letting her hand rest in his as he leaned in.

"Yeah, but still. I immediately felt something special as soon as I met you. I felt it right away. I know you're not supposed to say things like that to someone you've only met a few weeks ago, but with the ring and the dreams… I don't care."

The world around them had faded and the sounds of the café and the street were filtering to Netta as if through a gauze screen.

"My great aunt lives in Nicosia,"Thanos finally said. "Why don't we go there and check out her ring."

Netta sat back in her chair.

"I like that idea. Let's do it."

"Let me call her. She's always home but sometimes she goes over to a neighbor."

He pulled out his cell and rang his great aunt.

"Auntie Georgia," he said. "It's me, Thanos. Can I bring a friend over?"

He waited while she spoke to him.

"Yes, my friend and I are on our way. Are you going to be home?"

Thanos hung up the phone and turned to Netta.

"She's waiting for us," he said.

"You didn't tell her why we are visiting," Netta said.

"Well, yeah, I didn't. We'll talk to her when we get there."

Netta's mind was racing. Who was this man to her, whom she'd only met a few weeks ago but had such an effect on her psyche? There were too many points of connection to dismiss, but none of them made any sense. Any sense in conventional terms, that is. She'd always lived somewhat outside conventional society, with her strange visions and dreams haunting her mind. He seemed to be a kindred soul, someone who understood and even had dreams of his own. And what about seeing his face in her vision at Bellapais?

What was it that the gypsy had said? Something about Athanasios and Annie a long time ago. How did she know her name? Her mother called her Netta, short for Annie, her baptismal name. Her mother said it was a family name. What was the meaning of that? What was the shape of that time that loomed over her, whose mysterious tale she could only glimpse through fragments of visions, dreams, and emotions.

The two young people got back into the car and headed back towards Nicosia. They had both fallen silent, lost in their own thoughts.

As soon as they came to the outskirts of Limassol, the seashore appeared to their right.

"I can't believe the color of that water! I've never seen a sea so blue! It's beautiful."

Thanos smiled.

"Yes, it is. Guess I've gotten a little used to it and don't always appreciate it. It's nice to be reminded," he mused.

It wasn't long after they turned onto the highway to Nicosia. They arrived on the outskirts and then came into the center of town. His great aunt lived in one of the side streets of Old Nicosia where the homes were still low slung, in contrast to the new apartment buildings lining the road and the modern plaza at the city's bastion.

A woman wiping her hands on her apron was waiting for them at the front door. Her gray hair was cropped, and her skin bore the wrinkles of her years. They parked in her driveway. Her blue eyes twinkled as she greeted them, a warm embrace was her welcome.

"Thanos, my child! I'm so happy to see you." She turned to Netta. "And who's you're friend?' She took the girl's hand in both of hers.

Warmth seeped through Aunt Georgia's hands to Netta's. A warmth so profound and so deep she felt it reach her core.

Aunt Georgia gently touched Netta's chin.

"I feel like I've seen you before. Have you known Thanos long?" she asked, her cloudy eyes searching the young woman's face.

Netta was overwhelmed by the feelings that this woman's touch evoked. She was not unaccustomed to strange emotions or visions, yet this experience brought forth an ocean of feeling she didn't know what to do with.

She cupped the old woman's hand in hers. If she looked into her eyes long enough, maybe she could unspool the mystery that had troubled her ever since she could remember. She gently squeezed Aunt Georgia's hand. The old woman broke into a smile and released her.

As if coming out of a spell, Netta smiled awkwardly and followed Thanos inside while Georgia led them to the kitchen.

The smell of garlicky soup permeated the kitchen and a pot simmering on the stove was its obvious source. The small counters and the old terrazzo floors shone clean, and the toaster, old fridge and stove looked like they'd been the workers for many meals in that old house. A bowl of grapes sat on the kitchen table next to which a small demitasse cup of coffee was turned upside down in its little plate, a pool of dark coffee surrounding the rim.

"Reading your fortune, Aunt Georgia?" Thanos pointed to the cup mischievously.

The old woman tipped her head and gave a shy smile.

"It's out of habit, son," she said and motioned for them to sit.

"What can I get you?" she immediately asked, the Cyprus hospitality ingrained in her.

"We just had coffee," he replied. "Why don't you sit with us a bit." He pulled out a chair for her.

"I'm cooking lunch, and you must stay and eat. It's your favorite. Veal stew."

"Of course!" Thanos nodded looking at Netta.

"Yes, yes, of course," she quickly added.

Aunt Georgia sat at the table with them.

"My boy," she said and reached out to pat her nephew on the shoulder.

"Auntie," Thanos cleared his throat.

"Yes?"

"We wanted to talk to you about something,"

The old woman looked serene.

"Of course, ask me what you want."

The two young people exchanged a glance. Aunt Georgia turned from one to the other.

"Well, go on."

"Well, I remember you talking about a stone ring that we have in the family. I even saw it once. You and mom were looking at it and talking about some old story. I remember seeing it."

Aunt Georgia paused. She exhaled.

"I have been expecting you," she said looking at Netta. "I've been expecting you for a long time."

Netta's hair stood on end.

Aunt Georgia slowly rose from her chair and shuffled out of the kitchen. They heard her rummaging through drawers, and she finally emerged holding a weathered small wood box.

Aunt Georgia slowly lifted the lid.

There, in this simple old box, lay a stone ring. But not just any stone ring, but one so like the one she'd been given by her mother, Netta let out a small cry.

Aunt Georgia reached in and removed the ring from the box.

"Why did you want to see this ring?" she asked, offering it to Netta.

Netta's hand was in her pocket, wrapped around her ring. She pulled it out and showed it to Aunt Georgia.

Aunt Georgia's face lit up.

"I knew there was someone out there, I just knew it!" she cried.

"What are you talking about?"Thanos asked.

Aunt Georgia took a folded piece of paper from the bottom of the box. She opened it gently and smoothed it on the tabletop.

"This message has been in the box with the ring, handed down to us through the generations," she said." It's dated Fifteen Seventy-One."

"What does it say?"

"This stone ring was found on Ioannis in August of Fifteen Seventy-One, after the fall of Famagusta, when we found him on our doorstep, beaten unconscious and almost dead by the Ottoman soldiers. He never regained his memory. On his deathbed he asked for the ring and called out for Annie, Athanasios and Bellapais."

"Who is Ioannis?"Thanos asked.

"He is our ancestor," Aunt Georgia replied.

"How come I never heard of this before?" he asked puzzled.

"You have but were too young to pay attention. This has been in our family since the time of the fall of Famagusta to the Ottomans," she said.

He reached out and touched the paper. "But this is on paper, how could it have survived?" he paused. "And who is Annie?"

"I don't know who she is. As for the paper, you're right. Each generation has copied it onto a new sheet of paper to keep it going," she replied.

"My given name is Annie," Netta said, tentatively reaching for the ring. "Can I?" she asked.

"Of course," Aunt Georgia placed it in her hand.

A powerful wind blew through the open window as Netta held both rings in her hands. The kitchen door slammed shut. All three gasped at the electricity that permeated the air.

Netta set the rings down side by side, the one she'd brought smaller, fitting a woman's hand and the other one, large, as if for a man's finger. The stone fashioning both rings was a dark gray. The surfaces, uneven, appeared hand carved. No doubt, the rings were a pair, cut from the same stone, chiseled by the same carver.

"And Thanos' given name is Athanasios," Georgia said.

Thanos reached out and she placed the rings in his hands. His whole body trembled as he beheld the old rings. Aunt Georgia sat watching the two young people at her table. Netta and Thanos intertwined their fingers with each other across the kitchen table. Aunt Georgia got up and shuffled to her kitchen drawer. She returned, a red ribbon in her hand.

Without saying anything, she took the rings and tied each end of ribbon onto each one. She then placed each ring on the young couple's third finger, the red span of satin connecting them, as they joined hands again.

"In a Church wedding, we tie the rings with a red ribbon," she simply said.

Netta and Thanos sat there; hands clad in the stone rings of destiny, tethered to each other by the red ribbon of fate.

They looked up from the rings to each other's faces. The light coming through the kitchen window seemed brighter, their faces were lit with an aura, an inner glow, and it was as if the echoes of the past reached out to the present and illuminated the pair with centuries of promises and longing.

43 : Netta and Thanos

PRESENT TIME

Netta and Thanos left his Aunt Georgia's house trying to digest her revelations. They walked the darkened streets of old Nicosia, ducking into the courtyard of the chapel of Panagia Chrysalliniotissa. They strolled the covered archway around the old church, both lost in their own thoughts.

He squeezed her hand still bearing the stone ring, red ribbon untied and in Thanos' pocket.

She turned to look at him.

"What?" she smiled.

"That was a lot to take in today," he stopped walking.

"Yes," she replied looking down at her hands, playing with the ring.

"It feels right, Netta," he said. "It feels right."

She continued to look down at her hands.

"All my life, I've had these dreams; these visions that I didn't know what to do with. My mother would comfort me and say it was okay to have them. But I felt there was something different about me, different than the other children. I didn't understand what it was, but I learned to live with it."

"Yes," he encouraged her.

"Landing on this island, walking the grounds of Bellapais and mostly meeting you, have been the closest thing of making any sense of it."

"Yes!"

"Yet, with all the experiences that I've had, even for me these revelations from your aunt, the rings, it's a lot to absorb." She looked at him.

"For me too, Netta," he said. "When I first met you, I felt that there was something powerful drawing me to you. It was as if I had known you forever. I know it's crazy."

They stood wrapped in each other in the jasmine-scented night.

"It's like I've been waiting for you all my life," Netta said.

Thanos took her hands in his. He raised her right hand to his lips and kissed it.

"I promised I'd come for you, and here I am," he finally said to her.

Netta paused and stood there looking at him.

"You promised?" she questioned.

"I swear I don't know where that came from." He looked confused but earnest.

Netta's face remained pensive for a moment, until suddenly she broke into a soft smile.

"Yes, I remember. A long time ago, you promised me that you would come for me. I waited for a long time. But you're here now," she burrowed into his arms.

"We're together again, Netta," he whispered into her ear. "This land of ours, this small island in the middle of the Mediterranean has a long and eventful history. The echoes of the past are all around us, accompanying us at every step. Most of us, we don't feel it. We go about our lives, oblivious to all that history. Occasionally, the curtain is pulled, and some of us get a glimpse of the lives of our ancestors. I don't know anyone else who's had this experience. I do know that it's very real for me."

It certainly was real for Netta who'd lived with the mystique of this history, carrying it with her on her genetic code, encrypted through the ages with the lives and memories of her ancestors.

She took his hand, and they began to walk again around the small church.

As they slipped through the filigreed gate, the scent of jasmine intensified. Thanos stopped, leaned in and took her face in his hands. Netta, intoxicated by the history swirling around them, the ghosts of their ancestors cheering them on, and the perfume of jasmine blossoms that only last a night, surrendered herself to him in a long kiss.

They then walked back to their car through the narrow streets, where history reverberated through the centuries all around them, engulfing them in its violent bosom, at once comforting and unsettling.

Aerial photo of Bellapais Abbey

Interior Archways of Bellapais Abbey

Cloister View of Bellapais Abbey

www.ingramcontent.com/pod-product-compliance
Lightning Source LLC
LaVergne TN
LVHW020706110826
845149LV00012B/2136
* 9 7 8 0 9 9 1 5 7 9 6 3 1 *